"Why don't you just say in the first place that you are meeting me?"

"I like watching them fluster."

Kedah would like to see Felicia fluster, just a little, yet she was always so measured and poised and gave away so little of herself.

He would like to know more.

The thought surprised him. Kedah did not fraternize with his staff, yet over the past few weeks he had found himself wondering more and more about Felicia and what went on in her head.

It was a pretty head—one that was usually framed with shoulder-length hair but today it was worn up. It was too severe on her. Or was it that she'd lost a little weight? He could see that she'd put on some makeup in an attempt to hide the smudges under her eyes.

Gorgeous eyes, Kedah thought.

They regularly changed shade—today they were an inviting sea green but he would not be diving in.

One Night With Consequences

When one night...leads to pregnancy!

When succumbing to a night of unbridled desire it's impossible to think past the morning after!

But with the sheets barely settled, that little blue line appears on the pregnancy test and it doesn't take long to realize that one night of white-hot passion has turned into a lifetime of consequences!

Only one question remains:

How do you tell a man you've just met that you're about to share more than just his bed?

Find out in:

Look for more **One Night With Consequences**
coming soon!

Carol Marinelli

THE SHEIKH'S BABY SCANDAL

Recycling programs
for this product may
not exist in your area.

ISBN-13: 978-0-373-13465-6

The Sheikh's Baby Scandal

First North American publication 2016

Copyright © 2016 by Carol Marinelli

HARLEQUIN®
www.Harlequin.com

Printed in U.S.A.

Carol Marinelli recently filled in a form asking for her job title. Thrilled to be able to put down her answer, she put "writer." Then it asked what Carol did for relaxation and she put down the truth— "writing." The third question asked for her hobbies. Well, not wanting to look obsessed, she crossed her fingers and answered "swimming"—but given that the chlorine in the pool does terrible things to her highlights, I'm sure you can guess the real answer!

PROLOGUE

'KEDAH, WHERE ARE YOU? That's enough, now!'

The royal nanny was getting exasperated as she again called out to her small charge, but Kedah had no intention of being found—he was having far too much fun!

Kedah could see the nanny's feet go past as he hid behind the large statue that she had checked just a few seconds ago. He could run like greased lightning, and he smothered his laughter as she now moved towards the grand staircase.

'Kedah!' The nanny was sounding very cross. As well she might—Kedah was a handful.

The people of Zazinia adored him, though, and they would all be lined up outside the palace hoping to get a glimpse of him. Usually there was just a small crowd when the royal plane landed but, thanks to the cheeky young Prince, the numbers had grown of late.

Never had there been more interest in a young royal. Kedah's chocolate-brown eyes were flecked with gold and his winning smile had drawn rapt attention from the moment the first photographer had captured it. In their eyes he could do no wrong—in fact, Kedah's boisterous boyish ways only served to endear him further to the public. He was as beautiful as he was wild, they often said, and it would seem that he could not stand still.

He tried to!

For the people of Zazinia, a dreary parade was made so much more entertaining when they watched little Kedah's attempts to obey the stern commands that were delivered out of the side of his father's mouth.

Just a few weeks ago there had been a procession, and Kedah had had to remain still for the best part of an hour. But he had quickly grown bored.

'Control him!' Omar, the Crown Prince had said to Rina, his wife, for the King had started to get cross.

It was so hard to control him, though.

When his mother had warned him to stand still, Kedah had merely smiled up at her and then held out his arms to be lifted. Rina had tried to ignore him— but, really, who could resist? In the end she had complied. Kedah had chatted away to her, despite being gently hushed. She had smiled affectionately and put her hand up to his little fat cheek, looked him in the eye. She'd told him to behave for just a few more moments, and that then it would be time to return to the palace.

The King's silent disapproval had been felt all around. He did not approve of his son's young wife, and certainly he felt that children should be seen and not heard. Omar had been tense, Rina had done her best to appease all, and yet Kedah had chosen to be impervious to the strained atmosphere and turned his attention to the crowd.

They had all been staring at him, so he'd smiled and waved to them. It had been such a break from the usually austere and remote royal shows that the gathered crowd had melted *en masse* and, quite simply, adored him. Kedah was funny—and terribly cheeky. He had so much energy to burn that he was the work of five children, and the royal nanny struggled with this particular charge!

'Kedah!' she called out now, to thin air. 'I need to get you bathed and dressed so that you can go and greet your father and the King.'

He crouched lower behind the statue and did not respond. He was not particularly looking forward to the senior royals' return. They had been gone for a few days and the palace felt so much more relaxed without them. His mother seemed to laugh more, and even the staff were happier without the King around.

Neither did Kedah want to change out of his play clothes just so he could watch a plane land and his grumpy father and grandfather get out. And so, as the nanny sped down stairs in search of him, Kedah ran from behind the statue and tried to plan his next move.

Usually he would hide in the library, but on this day he ran somewhere he should not. Jaddi, his grandfather, had his own wing, and there were no guards there today—which meant that he was free to explore. But his eager footsteps came to a halt midway there. Even though his grandfather was away, Jaddi was intimidating enough that Kedah chose not to continue. And so, at the last moment, he changed his mind and turned and ran to the Crown Prince's wing, where his parents resided.

There were no guards there either.

To the left there were offices that ran the length of the corridor, and to the right was the entrance to his parents' private residence.

Kedah rarely entered it. His parents generally came and visited him in the nursery or the playroom.

Knowing that he would be told off if he disturbed his mother from her nap, for a second he considered the balcony—but then chose to run to the offices instead. He had long ago kicked off his sandals, so his bare feet made barely a sound.

Even though he was in a rush to find a hiding place, Kedah stopped for a moment and looked up at the portraits, as he always did when he was here.

They fascinated him.

He looked along the row of Crown Princes gone by. All were imposing-looking men, dressed in warrior robes with their hands on the hilt of their swords. All stared down at him with cool grey eyes and grim expressions.

He looked at a younger version of his grandfather, the King, and then he looked at his father.

They looked so stern.

One day, his mother had told him, *his* portrait would hang there, for he was born to be King. 'And you will be such a *good* king, Kedah. I know that you shall listen to your people.'

He had heard the brittle edge to his mother's voice as she'd gazed up at the portraits. 'Why don't they smile?' Kedah had asked.

'Because being Crown Prince is a serious thing.'

'I don't want it, then!' Kedah had laughed.

Now he looked away from the portraits and ran to a meeting room that had several desks. He went to hide under one, sure that he would not be found there.

Or perhaps he would, for there were noises coming from behind a large wooden door and he recognised his mother's voice as she called out. He knew that that was his father's private office, and wondered why she would be in there.

And then he heard a low cry.

It sounded as if his mother was hurt, and Kedah's expression changed from happy to a look of concern as he heard muffled sobs and moans.

His father had told him to take care of his mother while he was away. Even at this tender age, Kedah knew that people worried about her, for Rina could be unpredictable at times.

He came out from under the desk and stood wondering what he should do. He knew that the door handles were too high for him. For a moment he considered running to alert the royal nanny that his mother sounded distressed, but then he changed his mind. Often his mother wept, and it did not seem to endear her to the staff nor to the rest of the royal family.

And so, instead of getting help, Kedah selected a chair and started to drag it across the room. The chair was made of the same wood as the heavy door, and it felt like ages until he had got it close enough to climb upon it and attempt to turn the handle on the office door.

'Ummu…?' Kedah called out to his mother as he climbed onto the chair and turned the heavy handle. 'Ummu?' he said again as the door swung open.

But then he frowned, because his mother seemed to be sitting on the desk and yet she was being held in Abdal's arms.

'Intadihr!'

His mother shouted that Kedah was to stay where he was, and she and Abdal moved out of his line of sight. Kedah did as he was told. He was not sure what was happening, but a moment or so later Abdal walked past on his way out.

Kedah had never really liked him. Abdal was always cross whenever Kedah came to the offices and pleaded with his mother to take him for a walk. It was as if he didn't want the young Prince around.

Kedah stared at Abdal's departing back as the man walked quickly along the corridor and then, still standing on the chair, he turned and looked to his mother. Rina was flustered, and she smoothed down her robe as she walked towards him.

Kedah did not hold his arms out to be lifted. 'Why was Abdal here?' he asked. 'Where are the guards?'

There were no flies on Kedah—not even at that young age.

'It's okay,' Rina said as she lifted him, unyielding, from the chair. 'Mummy was upset and didn't want anyone to see. I was crying.'

'Why?' Kedah asked as he took in his mother's features. Her face was all red and, yes, he *had* heard her sob. 'Why are you always sad?'

'Because I miss my homeland sometimes, Kedah. Abdal is also from there. He is here to ease the transition and to help our two countries unite. Abdal understands how difficult it can be to get the King to agree to any changes. We were trying to come up with a way that will please all the people.'

Kedah just stared back at his mother as she hurriedly spoke on.

'Your father would be very upset if he knew that I had been crying while he was away. He is tired of arguing with the King and he has enough on his plate, so it is better not to tell him. It is better that you don't tell anyone what you just saw.'

Kedah stared into her eyes more deeply and tried to read her. His mother did not look sad. If anything, she looked scared, and that had his heart tightening in a fear for her that he didn't understand.

'I don't want you to be unhappy.'

'Then I shan't be,' Rina said, and brought a hand up to Kedah's face and cupped his taut cheek. 'After all, I have so much to give thanks for—I have a beautiful son and a wonderful home…'

'So don't you cry again,' Kedah said, and those gorgeous chocolate-brown eyes of his narrowed. He removed his mother's hand from his cheek and looked right into his mother's eyes. For one so very young, he spoke with command. *'Ever!'*

'Kedah, there you are…'

They both turned to the sound of the royal nanny's voice, and he did not understand why the nanny stammered and blushed as she apologised to Her Royal Highness for losing sight of her young charge.

'I've been looking for him all over the palace.'

'It's fine,' Rina said, handing Kedah over. 'We'll say no more about it.'

A little while later his father and the King returned, and life went as before.

Kedah continued to be boisterous, and yet from that day there was a defiant edge to his antics. From then on those brown eyes narrowed if anyone got too close. He kept his own counsel and he trusted no one.

A few years later his brother was born and that signalled happier times, for Mohammed was a model child.

Weary of the wilder young Prince, the King insisted he be schooled overseas, and little Kedah attended a boarding school in London. He somehow knew that he held a secret that, if ever revealed, might well destroy not only the people he loved but the kingdom his family ruled.

And as he matured Kedah knew how dire the consequences would be for his mother. If her infidelity was exposed she would be shamed, and the King would have no choice but to divorce her and separate her from her sons.

But secrets had ways of seeping out through even the most heavily guarded walls. Servants gossiped amongst themselves as children played at their feet, and royal nannies eventually married and indulged in pillow talk of their own. Rumours spread wide when they were carried on desert winds—and returned multiplied, of course.

And as Kedah grew, and returned to Zazinia during term breaks, the portraits fascinated him for a different reason.

Perhaps what was being said was true and he was *not* his father's son. After all, he looked nothing like any of them.

But his doubts were not because of the rumours that refused to fade with the passage of time—Kedah knew what he had seen.

CHAPTER ONE

YOU NEED FELICIA HAMILTON.

Crown Prince Sheikh Kedah of Zazinia had always made sure that he needed no one.

He was reliant only on himself.

That late afternoon he sat in his London office and rolled a rare spherical diamond between the pads of his index finger and thumb as he read a newspaper article on his computer. When there was a knock on the door and he called for Anu to come in he saw that she looked rather tense. He wondered if she had read the article too.

What was being discussed in it would distress her, he knew. She had been a loyal member of his team for a number of years and was also from his homeland. She would understand how damning this article was.

'Ms Hamilton is here for her interview,' Anu said, and her lips pursed a little.

'Send her in, then.'

'She asked for a few moments to freshen up.'

Oh, Anu tried, but she could not hold her pro-

tests in. All the staff who came into contact with
Kedah had a preliminary interview with Anu first.
Yesterday she had met with Felicia, and found the
young woman did not tick any of the usual boxes that
might get her through to a second round interview.
She lacked hospitality experience—though she made
up for it in attitude—and that would *never* do when
working for Kedah. He was not exactly known for
consulting with his staff. He had a packed schedule
and he expected his team to work quietly and seamlessly in the background—which was something Anu
could not see happening with Miss Hamilton.

Anu had reported this to him yesterday, and yet
Kedah had told her to call Felicia back and invite her
to come in this afternoon.

'Kedah, I really don't think that she is suitable to
work as your PA.'

'Anu, I understand that you have concerns, and
they have been noted. Can you please alert me when
Miss Hamilton decides that she is ready?'

As the door closed behind Anu, Kedah replaced
the diamond in the inside pocket of his jacket and returned to the news article that he had been reading.

It was in English. No one from his homeland
would dare to publish such a piece. Not yet.

Heir (not so) Apparent!

Beneath the daring title there was a picture of
Kedah, wearing a suit and tie and a rich, arrogant

smile. It spoke of the recent death of Kedah's grand-father and how, now that Omar was King, certain difficult topics needed to be raised. It briefly discussed Kedah's British education and subsequent jet-set lifestyle and playboy reputation. It mentioned how, at thirty, he still showed no sign of settling down.

The article also spoke about his younger brother Mohammed and his wife Kumu and their two sons. Unlike Kedah, Mohammed had been schooled in Zazinia, and there was a considerable faction in the country who considered that, for stability, Mohammed would make a more suitable Crown Prince and subsequent King. The article stated that some of the elders were now calling for the Accession Council to meet and for a final decision to be made.

At the end of the piece there was a photo of Mohammed and Omar, but most damning of all was the caption below: *Like Father, Like Son.*

Apart from the years that separated them, Mohammed and Omar were identical—not just in looks but in their staid, old-fashioned ways.

The only change that Omar had made while Crown Prince had been an update to the education system. Over the years Kedah had made no progress with his father either. Kedah was a highly skilled architect, yet every design he'd submitted had been rejected and every suggestion he'd made either immediately turned down or later overruled.

He had hoped, now that his grandfather was dead,

that things might change, but his latest proposal for a stunning waterfront hotel and shopping complex had been rejected too.

His father had pointed out that the new building would look onto the private royal beach.

'There are ways around that,' Kedah had insisted. 'If you would just let me—'

'The decision is final, Kedah,' the King had interrupted. 'I have discussed it at length with the elders…'

'And you have discussed it at length with Mohammed,' Kedah had said. 'I hear that he was *very* vocal in his criticism of my plans.'

'I listen to all sides.'

'Well, you should listen to me first,' Kedah had said. 'Mohammed is *not* the Crown Prince.'

'Mohammed is the one who is here.'

'I have told you—I will not live in Zazinia if I am to be ineffectual.'

Kedah turned off his computer so he did not have to see the offensive article.

Earlier today, when it had first appeared, he had called Vadia, his assistant in Zazinia, and had been assured that it would be pulled down from the internet. There was no denying, though, that things were coming to a head. Even before their grandfather's death Mohammed had decided that *he* would make a better Crown Prince and future King. Many of the elders thought the same, and—as the article had stated—there was a strong push for a meeting of the Accession Council to discuss the future of the royal family formally.

His father would have the final say, but rather than declaring outright that he would prefer his younger son to be King one day, Omar seemed to be pushing Kedah into stepping aside.

Kedah refused to.

Instead he was busy making plans.

He had many rich and influential friends, and he knew a lot of bad boys too. Matteo Di Sione was both. He had a reputation that rivalled even Kedah's.

They had met up in New York a couple of weeks ago—and not by chance. Kedah hadn't told Matteo the issue, just that he was expecting turbulent times ahead and needed someone tough who could handle things. Matteo had made some discreet enquiries on his friend's behalf and had come back to Kedah with his findings.

You need Felicia Hamilton.

Kedah glanced at the time. Usually a potential employee who arrived late for an interview and then asked for time to freshen up wouldn't even make it through the door of his office.

What the *hell* was she doing? he wondered.

She was reading.

Felicia hadn't actually *intended* to keep Sheikh Kedah waiting for quite so long. The West End was gridlocked—thanks to a red carpet awards show taking place tonight, the taxi driver had told her. So Felicia, sitting in the back and doing some final research on Kedah on her way to the interview, had decided to walk the last couple of blocks. But then a very interesting article had turned up on her tablet and, after arriving at his impressive office, she'd wanted a few more moments to go through it.

Now perhaps she understood why she had been called back after that disastrous interview yesterday. Anu had spoken to her as if Felicia wanted to *work* for Kedah—a real job, so to speak—and after an awkward twenty minutes, during which it had become increasingly clear that Felicia was not the type Sheikh Kedah employed, the two women had parted ways.

Still, her phone had rung this morning and Felicia had smiled to herself when she had been invited to return and meet with the man himself. Of course Kedah didn't want a PA—it was her troubleshooting skills he required.

Now she knew why!

It would seem that Crown Prince Sheikh Kedah of Zazinia was fighting for the throne—and Felicia was now sure he wanted to commence the clean-up of his reputation.

From what she knew of him, it would take more than industrial strength bleach!

If there was a scale for playboys, then Kedah was at the extreme top. In fact his partying ways were legendary.

How the mighty fell!

Today this oh, so arrogant man would reveal his troubles to Felicia. Of course she would look suitably unshocked as he did so, and assure him that whatever trouble he was in she could sort it.

Felicia was *very* good at her job because she had been doing it all her life.

She had been taught to smile for the cameras alongside Susannah, her long-suffering mother, long before she could even walk. She had on many occasions sat in the family lounge with spin doctors and PR people as they had debated how her father's multiple affairs and the trashy headlines and exposés should best be dealt with.

There had even been times when they had come to her school. Felicia could remember sitting in the headmaster's office with her parents, being reminded that cameras would be on them when they left. She had been told what to do as they walked, as a family, to the waiting car.

'Remember to smile, Felicia.'

'Susannah, hold his hand as you walk to the car and don't forget to laugh when he whispers to you.'

And her mother had done as she was told. Susannah had done everything that had been asked of her. But in the end it had all been to no avail. When Felicia was fourteen her father had decided to update to a younger model and had walked out on them.

A legal wrangle had ensued.

The lovely private boarding school that had been such a haven for her had disappeared when the school fees hadn't been paid, and with it had gone Felicia's friends and her beloved pony.

Susannah had fallen apart, and it had been up to her daughter to be strong. They had rented a small house while waiting for the money to be sorted out and Felicia had enrolled in the local school—but she hadn't fit in. Her dreams of being a vet had long gone by then, and she'd left school at sixteen. She had taken an office job to help with the rent.

Those days were gone now.

Felicia was highly sought-after, and her trouble-shooting talents were coveted by the rich and famous. Her mother lived in a house that Felicia had bought and paid for, and Felicia owned her own flat.

Some questioned how she could defend these men—but, really, Felicia was just doing what she'd been taught.

The only difference was that now she was paid.

And paid handsomely.

She ran a comb through her dark blonde hair, touched up her lip gloss and added a slick of mascara to bring out the green of her eyes. As she headed out Anu told her to take a seat. Guessing the newspaper article would soon be taken down, she took a few quick screenshots on her phone as Sheikh Kedah now kept *her* waiting.

Oh, well! She had done the same to him.

Working with this type of man, Felicia had found that it was terribly important to establish early on that *his* ego had to be put aside and that from this point on *she* ran the show. It was even more vital to establish that they weren't suddenly best friends and, given the reputations of the men she dealt with, to make it clear they would never be lovers.

Felicia would be very nice at first, of course, while he told her what was going on, but then her smile would fade and she'd tell him what had to be done if he wanted to come out of this intact.

The truth was that Felicia despised these men.

She just knew, from wretched experience, how to deal with them.

'You might want to put your phone away,' Anu suggested.

Felicia was about to decline politely when a rich, deep and heavily accented voice spoke for her.

'I'm sure Ms Hamilton is just keeping up to date with the news.'

She looked up.

She had prepared thoroughly for this moment— determined not to let such a superfluous thing as his stunning looks sideswipe her. She had examined many photos to render herself immune to him. Only no photograph could fully capture the beauty of Sheikh Kedah in the flesh.

He was wearing an exquisitely cut dark suit and tie, but they were mere details for she had little interest in his attire. And it was not the caramel of his skin against his white shirt or his thick glossy black hair that forced her to try to remember to breathe. Nor was it cheekbones that looked as if Michelangelo himself had spent a couple of days sculpting them to perfection. Even sulky full lips that did not smile hardly mattered, for Felicia was caught in the trap of his eyes.

They were thickly lashed and a rich shade of chocolate-brown with golden flecks and—unlike most of her clients—he met her gaze steadily.

Oh, she was *extremely* good at her job. For, despite the jolt to her senses, Felicia did not let her reaction reveal itself to him and instead stood up, utterly composed.

'Come through,' he said.

And she smiled.

Widely.

She had a smile that took men's breath away. It was a smile so seemingly open that hardened reporters would thrust their microphones a little closer and their lenses would zoom in, so certain were they that it would waver.

It never did.

And long ago she had trained herself not to blush.

'I'm sorry I'm late,' Felicia said as she walked towards him. 'The traffic was terrible.'

He almost forgave her, for in turn Felicia was not what Kedah had been expecting. He had thought, given she had been invited for a formal second interview, that she would be in a suit, but Felicia looked rather more like a lady who lunched and was wearing a pretty off-white dress.

It was fitted enough that it showed her slender frame and pert bust, while short enough to reveal her toned legs. She was wearing high-heeled strappy sandals and looked nothing like the hard-nosed woman he had been prepared for. In fact she was as delicate-looking as she was pretty. She was so soft and smiling that Kedah was quite sure Matteo had got it all wrong.

Felicia Hamilton was the very *last* person he needed. Moreover, she was exactly the soft and submissive type he desired!

Naturally he had looked her up and had seen a picture of her in a boxy suit with her hair worn up. She had been coming out of court, with a terribly famous and thoroughly disgraced sportsman by her side. She had spoken for him and her voice had been crisp and to the point.

Today Kedah had expected brittle, and yet there was a softness to her that confused him. Her hair was long and layered and framed a heart-shaped face, and her fragrance was light and floral, meeting his nostrils as he held the door open for her and she passed him.

'Please…' Kedah gestured. 'Take a seat.'

Felicia did so, placing her bag by her side and crossing her legs at the ankles. Though he seemed utterly composed, Felicia was prepared for anything. Often the door had barely closed before her future client broke down. *'For God's sake, Felicia, you have to help me!'* they all too often begged. *'You have to stop this from getting out!'*

Yes—*client*.

Oh, she might call them her boss when she was in front of the camera lens but, as Kedah would soon find out, it was Felicia who was in charge.

Yet instead of begging for her help Kedah calmly offered refreshments.

'No, thank you.'

'You're sure?' he checked.

'Quite sure. I had a late lunch.'

And his troubles would be a very sweet dessert!

He walked around the desk and took his place and Felicia ran a tongue over her glossed lips as she waited for him to reveal the salacious truth.

'You come highly recommended.'

'Thank you.'

'Ms Hamilton?' he checked. 'Or can I call you Felicia?'

'Felicia's fine,' she offered. 'How would you like me to address *you*?'

'Kedah.'

She nodded.

They went through the formalities. He told her he was an esteemed architect, which of course she already knew.

'I used to sell them off, but now once I design a hotel I tend to hold on to it,' Kedah explained needlessly.

She just wished he'd get to the point.

'So I have a fleet of hotels across the world, which in turn means I have a lot of staff...'

Felicia nodded and wished they could lose the charade and get to the good bit.

'Do you have much experience in the hospitality industry?' he asked.

Felicia frowned. She'd expected a confessional—to sit, seemingly non-judgmental, as he poured out his past—yet he seemed to be actually interviewing her.

'Not really. Though of course I've stayed in an awful lot of hotels!'

Oh, she had. And if Kedah was going on word of mouth then he'd know that she worked for just a few weeks a year.

He didn't even deign to smile at her small joke.

'As I hope Anu explained, the role would involve extensive travel. If you work for me the hours will be very long. Sometimes there are eighteen-hour days. If we are away you would also work weekends. Do you have other commitments?'

'My current employer is my only commitment,' Felicia answered. It was the truth—whatever his crisis, it would have her full attention.

'Good.' Kedah nodded. 'How soon would you be able to start?'

'As soon as the contract is signed.' Felicia smiled. 'I trust Anu gave you my terms?'

'Indeed she did.'

Felicia Hamilton commanded quite a fee.

'What about your personal life?' he asked.

'That's not your concern,' Felicia answered.

'Be sure to keep it that way,' Kedah said. 'I don't want to hear that your boyfriend is upset because you missed his birthday, or that your mother-in-law has surgery next week and you need some time off. Care factor? Zero.'

Felicia's response was to laugh, and for once it was genuine. Honesty had been somewhat lacking in her life, and she would far prefer the truth than a dressed-up lie.

And now she waited—*how* she waited—for that cool facade to crack and for Kedah to admit that he had royally stuffed up and needed his past to disappear. But instead he spoke of hotels and designs, and she stifled a yawn as he told her about Hussain, a graphic designer he regularly used.

'He's excellent. He actually studied with my father many years ago. We have worked on many designs together—mainly in the UAE.'

Felicia stifled another yawn.

'Why don't I show you some examples of my work—as well as a few of the hotels we shall be visiting in the coming weeks?' Kedah said, and then dimmed the lights.

Felicia wondered for a brief second if refreshments might be in order after all. Was she about to get a private screening of the trouble Sheikh Kedah was in? A steamy sex tape? The Crown Prince bound and gagged in a seedy encounter, perhaps?

Kedah watched that tongue pop out and moisten

those lovely lips as she sat straight in the chair, giving him her full attention.

Then he smiled unseen as her shoulders slumped and she sat through the forty-minute presentation that took her through some of his luxury hotels. She fought to keep her eyes from crossing as she watched it.

What the hell...?

'Do you have any questions?' Kedah invited as he flicked on the lights.

No! She just wanted him to cut to the chase and reveal the truth. 'Not at this stage,' she said.

'There must be things that you want to ask me?' he invited. 'Surely you have come prepared? You will have looked me up?'

'Of course I have.'

'What do you think your role might entail?' he asked as he went through her file.

Maybe he was shy, Felicia thought. Though that made no sense. He looked far from shy. But perhaps he needed a little help revealing his dark truths, so she decided to broach things gently. 'I would guess, from my research, that I'll be running a dating agency with only one man on the books,' Felicia said, and watched him closely for a reaction.

Kedah merely looked up from the papers and stared back at her as she continued.

'Though of course rather more discreetly than my predecessors.'

'Discreetly?' Kedah frowned.

'You tend to hit the glossies rather a lot.'

'That's hardly my staff's fault.'

'Well, they should monitor what's said. If a woman's upset…'

'As far as my sex life goes, you would just have to deal with the bookings and the brochure, Felicia…'

'Brochure?

He didn't enlighten her. 'What I am saying is that you do *not* police comments or apologise on my behalf. I am quite grateful for "the glossies", as you call them, for if women expect anything more from me than a night in bed, possibly two, then that is their own foolish mistake. They cannot say they haven't been duly warned.'

No, not shy, Felicia decided as he continued to speak.

'But I do expect discretion from all who work for me. Naturally you will have to sign a confidentiality agreement.'

'I told Anu yesterday that I shan't.'

Kedah, who had gone back to going through the papers, glanced up.

'Nobody would employ a PA without one.'

'If you look through my references you'll see that they do.' She gave him a smile, as if she was asking if he took sugar with his coffee—one lump or two? 'You either trust me or you don't.'

'I don't,' he responded. 'Though please don't take it personally. I don't trust anyone.'

'Good, because neither do I.'

Kedah was fast realising there was nothing apart from her appearance that was delicate. She was actually rather fascinating, and any doubts he might have had about her being up to the job were starting to fade.

He had no intention of telling her his situation just yet, of course, but he had decided that he wanted her onside. 'We can't go any further without you signing one.'

'Well, we can't go any further, then,' she said, and reached for her bag.

He didn't halt her.

'Thank you for wasting my time,' she added, and gave him another flash of that stunning smile.

Kedah noted that it didn't quite reach her eyes. They were a dazzling emerald-green—a shade that was one of a forest reflected on a lake…emerald, yet glacial.

He watched, quietly amused, as she began to flounce off.

'Sit down, Felicia.'

There was such command to his tone that it stopped her.

His voice wasn't remotely raised. If anything his words were delivered with an almost bored calm. But he might as well have reached for a lasso, for it was as if something had just wrapped around her. Oh, Felicia *heard* his words—yet she *felt* them at the base of her spine, and it tingled as he continued speaking.

'I haven't finished with you yet.'

CHAPTER TWO

IF EVER A voice belonged in the bedroom, it was Kedah's.

Not just a bedroom.

A boardroom would do nicely too.

For the second time in an hour Felicia was transported to that headmaster's office—but it was a far nicer version this time!

He was utterly potent. She almost wanted to keep walking towards the door, just for the giddy pleasure of finding out that she had a scruff to her neck as he hauled her back.

What she could not know was that the very controlled Sheikh Kedah was actually thinking along the same lines.

Felicia was absolutely his type.

He stared at the back of her head and then took in her rigid shoulders, let his dark eyes run the length of her spine. Her face was heart-shaped, and so too were her buttocks, and his eyes rested there for a moment too long.

Then he forced them away.

Kedah did not need the complication of a fake PA who turned him on.

He liked softness on his pillow and sweet, batting eyes, and he didn't care if his women lied as they simpered.

It was, after all, just a game.

And then he thought of the games he might play with Felicia.

He wanted to haul her to his knee and give her the job description as he ravished that mouth.

Know my hotels inside out, meet my staff, handle the press, and keep my world floating as I fight for my title. Now, let's go to bed.

Of course he did not say that.

This was business, and Kedah was determined it would remain so.

'Take a seat,' he said.

Felicia breathed out through her nostrils as he mentally undressed her. She felt as if he had even seen what colour knickers she had on. Flesh-coloured, actually. Not because she was boring, she wanted to hasten to add, but because of the white dress.

Oh, help!

And though common sense told her to leave now, to get out while she still could and most definitely should, neither had Felicia finished with *him*.

She wanted to know why he'd brought her here. She was positive that he didn't really want her working as his PA. So she turned around.

'Why are you so against signing a confidentiality agreement?' he asked, in such a measured tone that Felicia wondered if she'd misread the crackling tension.

'They're pointless.' She fought for professionalism and cleared her throat as the interview resumed. 'If, as you've stated, you trust no one, then a confidentiality agreement, no matter how watertight, cannot protect you.'

'It offers some level of security.'

'Well, it doesn't for me,' Felicia responded. 'What if something is leaked and you assume that *I* was the source?'

He didn't answer.

'I'm pretty unshockable, but what if you do something abhorrent?' she challenged. 'Am I supposed to turn a blind eye just because I've signed up for silence?'

'I'm bad,' Kedah said. 'Not evil.'

That made her smile, and this time it reached those stunning cold eyes.

'Sit down,' he said again. 'We can discuss it at the end of your trial.'

'There's nothing further to discuss on that subject—and also I don't do trials.' Felicia did sit down again, though. 'A one-year contract is the minimum I'll sign.'

'I might not need you for a year.'

That was the first real hint that there *was* more going on here. Maybe he felt awkward about telling her about his past—but that made no sense. There was nothing chaste about that blistering gaze. Perhaps there was something big about to come out? A huge scandal about to hit?

Felicia was tired of playing games. She wanted to know what she was getting into before she signed.

'Kedah, I'm not a defence lawyer.'

He simply stared back at her as she spoke, and she thought that never before had she had a client so able to meet her gaze.

'You *can* tell me whatever it is that's going on.'

Still he said nothing.

'I'm quite sure I already know.'

'Do tell,' he offered.

'I think you need me to restore your reputation,' she told him. 'And I can. Let me get to work, and in a matter of weeks I'll have you looking like an altar boy,'

'I hope not.'

'So do I...'

She faltered. Her voice had dropped to a smoky level that had no place at work—actually no place in her *life* till this point. Felicia dated, but she preferred the safe comfort of feeling lukewarm to this feeling of being speared on the end of a fondue stick and dipped at his whim.

She cleared her throat. 'Well, an altar boy might be pushing things, but if there's anything you're worried about...'

'Worrying is a pointless pursuit—and, as I thought

I'd made clear, I'm fine with my reputation,' Kedah answered smoothly, and although his expression did not display even a trace of amusement Felicia felt as if he was laughing at her. 'In fact I've loved every minute that I've spent earning it.'

Kedah was entranced, for Felicia hadn't so much as blinked, nor had she blushed, and he decided then that she was hired.

'Okay, no confidentiality agreement. But mess with me, Felicia, and I will deal with you *outside* of the law.'

Now she blushed—but at a point far lower on her body than her face. She was about to make some glib comment about being tipped over his knee but rather rapidly changed her mind.

'Six months,' Kedah said.

'A year,' she refuted. 'And when I'm no longer needed you pay out the rest of my contract and I'll be on my way.'

'Is that what generally happens?' For a moment he let his guard drop—just a little. He was curious about her job. Fascinated, in fact. 'You do a few weeks' work for a year's pay?'

She nodded and Kedah—albeit briefly—forgot his own dark troubles. He wanted to know more, but Felicia shook her head when he asked.

'I don't discuss my previous clients, and of course I'll provide you with that same courtesy.' Her voice sounded a little frantic now. 'Now you need to tell me what's going on if I'm to do my job.'

'Felicia,' he offered, in a rather bored drawl, 'I didn't hire you to tidy up my reputation. This leopard shan't be changing his spots. I want a PA and I hear that you're amongst the best. Do you want the role or not?'

Her smile slipped and those once glacial eyes clouded in confusion.

He pushed forward the contract.

'We need to discuss terms and conditions,' Kedah explained, and then went through them.

Basically, for the next year she was his.

Well, not *his*!

Just at his beck and call. Even if he was in Zazinia without her she would be working here.

There would be no reprieve.

Felicia wondered if now was the time to state, as she usually did, that she never slept with clients.

She looked at his long slender fingers as they turned the page and moved on to remuneration.

'Regarding your salary...' he said.

'Kedah.'

She watched as with a stroke of his pen he doubled it.

'I expect devotion.'

Now! she thought. He had given the perfect opening, Felicia knew. Right now she should smile and nod as she warned him that there were certain things out of bounds.

And there were.

Of course there were.

But actually to state that nothing could possibly happen might make her a liar. Even if *he* didn't, Felicia trusted her own word, so she refrained from her usual terse speech.

He crossed out the confidentiality clause, and initialled it, and then it was time for them both to countersign.

Felicia read through the contract again, and noted that her starting date was today.

Now.

'Kedah…' Felicia felt it only fair to warn him. 'I don't think I'll make a very good PA.'

'On the contrary,' he said. 'I think you'll be excellent.'

There was more to this.

Quite simply, there had to be.

And Felicia wanted to know what it was.

With a hand that somehow remained steady she used her own pen to sign her name and initial in all the right places and that was it—she was tied to him for a year.

Unfortunately not literally.

'Why are you laughing?' he asked, when she suddenly did.

'Just something I said in my head.' Felicia replied, and tried to right herself.

She looked out of the window to a bosky summer evening and knew the rush Kedah gave her was a giddy one. She wanted to go home now, to collect her thoughts.

'I'm looking forward to working with you, Kedah,' Felicia said, and held out her hand to shake his.

'Good,' he said, but did not shake her hand.

It became suddenly clear she was not dismissed.

'Anu will show you to your office. I believe my assistant in Zazinia will be free to speak with you in an hour.'

'I thought...' she started. But, as she was about to find out, the interview was over, the negotiations were done, and Kedah had nothing more to discuss.

'That will be all for now.'

It would seem that at five p.m. on a Friday her work day had just begun.

The gorgeous office would tomorrow have Felicia's name on its door, Anu told her, and there was an award-winning chef a phone call away who would prepare whatever she chose for supper.

And so she got busy.

It was late in Zazinia but Vadia, Kedah's assistant there, looked fresh and crisp on the video link.

'The offending article has been taken down,' she informed Felicia. 'If you could let Kedah know that?'

So she didn't use his title when she spoke of him either, Felicia thought as Vadia continued.

'I am trying to schedule the finishing touches on his official portrait. The artist is due to go overseas for surgery in a couple of months' time, so if you could tell Kedah that it is becoming rather pressing?'

'I shall.'

Then she went through his upcoming agenda, and it was so full that Felicia wondered how on earth he'd had the time to earn his reputation.

'I shall speak with you again tomorrow.' Vadia smiled.

Tomorrow was Saturday. Not that a little thing like the weekend seemed to matter in Kedah's world.

'If you can just push Kedah for an answer regarding the artist? Also remind him that the next time he's home we will be arranging the date for his bridal selection.'

As easily as that Vadia slipped it in. In fact she spoke as if she was trying to pin him down for a dental appointment.

'Bridal selection?' Felicia checked.

'Kedah knows.' Vadia smiled again. 'Just inform him that his father, the King, wants a date.'

As Vadia disappeared from the screen Felicia sat for a moment, trying to assimilate all she had found out today. While Kedah might insist that his reputation wasn't an issue, it might prove to be one for any future bride.

Especially if said reputation continued unchecked.

Was that why she was here? Felicia pondered. Was he soon to marry and she was to take charge of his social life here in England?

No way.

Felicia was used to putting out fires—not sitting back and watching them be lit.

* * *

Anu was the gatekeeper to Kedah's office, and as Felicia walked over to ask her something she saw that she was happily taking her supper break and eating a fragrant meal as she watched the awards show live on the computer.

'Oh, she won!' Anu smiled and put down her cutlery, and clapped as Felicia came to her side and watched a pretty young actress take her place on the stage. 'She's such a lovely person,' Anu said. 'Just genuinely nice!'

Please! Felicia thought, about to point out to Anu that actresses *acted*, and that was what Miss Pretty was doing right now as she thanked everyone—absolutely everyone…not just God, but her neighbour's blind cat too—in her little breathless voice.

'She's just acting…' Felicia started, and was about to say what a load of whitewash it all was when Kedah stalked out of his office. 'I was about to come in and speak with you,' Felicia said. 'Vadia needs some dates—'

'Not now,' he interrupted. 'Felicia, can you find out what after-party Beth will be attending and get me on the list? And could you also call The Ritz and have them prepare my suite?'

'Beth?' Felicia frowned.

'The actress who just won that award,' Kedah said.

'Do you know her?' she asked, but he had already disappeared.

'Not yet.' Anu smirked as she answered for him.

And the oddest thing of it all was that Anu didn't seem bothered one bit. Anu—who had looked as if she was chewing lemons all through Felicia's interview—didn't seem to mind in the least about Kedah's wild ways.

The staff at The Ritz were also clearly more than used to him. His suite was already prepared, Felicia found out when she called. And the organisers of the after-party would be delighted to add him to the list. In fact they asked if they could send a car.

'I'm not sure,' Felicia said. 'Can I call you back?'

'Just check with him,' Anu suggested, and gestured to his door for Felicia to go in. 'Though I doubt he'll want one.'

Felicia knocked and entered and there Kedah was—all showered and cologned, as sexy as sin, as he pulled on a fresh shirt and she got her first glimpse of a heavenly brown and broad chest. Michelangelo had clearly been at that, she thought, as she tried and failed not to notice the fan of silky straight black hair. Straight? Yes, straight, Felicia realised as she glanced down to where his trousers sat low on his hips.

'The party is all ready for you,' Felicia said, managing not to clear her throat. 'They offered to send a car.'

'Tell them no. I prefer to use my own transport.'

'Sure.'

His shirt was now done up, and he frowned as he

pulled out a tie and saw that Felicia remained. 'Can you call down for my driver?'

'Of course,' Felicia said. 'But can we quickly discuss a couple of things? Vadia needs a date for your portrait to be finished and also to arrange your bridal selection.' She watched for his reaction, for Kedah to falter and possibly tell her the real reason she was here, but instead he finished knotting his tie and pulled on his jacket.

'We can go through all that another time. I'll see you tomorrow.'

He had that hunter's look in his eye, and Felicia guessed there was no point talking business now.

Nor brides.

'Hey, Kedah!' she called as he went to walk off.

'What?' His reply was impatient—there was an after-party for him to get to after all.

'I don't think Beth *is* actually that nice,' she said, and on his way out he halted. In a matter of fact voice, she explained better. 'Usually I warn my clients if I think they're courting trouble…'

Now she had his attention, and she watched as he turned around and walked over to where she stood. She'd expected a question, for him to ask for a little more of what she knew about the woman, but he came right over and faced her, stepped into her personal space.

Too close?

He was a decent distance away, and there was nothing intimidating about his stance, yet her body was on high alert and his fragrance was heavy on her senses. Without saying so, he demanded that her eyes meet his.

'I'm not your *client*, Felicia,' he said, in a voice that held warning. 'I'm your boss. Got it?'

And she stood there, prickling and indignant, as he put her very firmly in her place.

'I was just trying to—'

'I don't need warnings,' he said. 'And, between you and me, I've already guessed that Beth is not *nice*. My intention tonight is to prove it.'

Then he smiled.

Oh, it was a real smile.

Her first!

It stretched his lips and it warmed her inside. It was like ten coffees on waking and it was the moment Felicia discovered the skin behind her knees—because it felt as if he were stroking her there with his long slender fingers, even though his hands were held at his side.

'Goodnight, Felicia. It was a pleasure to meet you and I'm looking forward to *working* with you.'

She heard the emphasis on the word working and let out a slightly shrill laugh. 'Fair enough.' She put her hands up as if in defence. 'You don't need another mother...'

'I certainly don't.'

'But know this,' Felicia said, and delivered a warning of her own. 'I shan't be arranging hotels and after-parties once you've chosen your wife.'

He stared at her for the longest time, even opened his mouth to speak, but then he changed his mind.

Kedah did not have to explain himself—and certainly not to a member of staff.

Which Felicia *was*, he reminded himself.

And a member of staff she would remain, for there were plenty of actresses and supermodels to be had.

'Be here at seven-thirty tomorrow and don't be late.'

He stalked out of the office. There was no slamming of the door—he didn't even bother to close it—but she was as rattled as if he'd banged it shut.

Oh, she would *not* fall for him.

Yes, if there was a scale for playboys then Kedah would be at the extreme end. The problem was Felicia could easily see why.

It was impossible not to want him.

It was the first time she'd realised she must heed her mother's advice.

'Never fall for a bastard. Especially not one who can make you smile.'

And Kedah did.

Oh, he most certainly did.

CHAPTER THREE

FELICIA BRISKLY MADE her way along Dubai's The
Walk, towards the restaurant she had booked for their
lunchtime meeting. There was no time to linger, or
to take in the delicious view. Kedah's multiple assistants were kept far too busy for that.

At the age of twenty-six, Felicia Hamilton had
a job.

A *real* one.

Instead of her regular four weeks or so of work
for a full year's pay, and a long pause between jobs,
Felicia now found herself working the most ridicu-
lous hours as she travelled the globe with Kedah.
Oh, their mode of transport was luxurious—Kedah
had his own private jet—but even a mile up in the
air there was little downtime. Kedah considered his
jet another office, and it was the same at his luxurious hotels.

She'd never have agreed to a year of this had she
known.

Except not only had she agreed to it—Felicia herself had been the one to insist on it. He had told her

exactly what to expect at the interview. He'd even offered her a trial period, which she'd declined!

Oh, what a fool. Had she taken the trial then she would have been finishing up by now!

Or would she…?

Even after close to eight weeks spent working hard for him Felicia still didn't believe that Kedah just wanted her as a PA.

She wasn't even very good at it.

Felicia was the one who generally gave orders. Now each day she stared down the barrel of her to-do list, as did his other assistants. One PA would never be enough for him.

There had to be another reason she was here.

Felicia was trying hard to work it out, but really there was little time for daydreaming. Her schedule was relentless.

She was up at six each day, and it was often close to midnight before she crashed—just as Kedah hit the town with his sweet and oh, so pleasing date of choice for the night.

Felicia honestly didn't know how he did it.

Since meeting him she was on her second lot of concealer, to hide the shadows under her eyes.

There had been a tiny reprieve last night. Kedah had asked her to book theatre tickets for himself and his latest bimbo—which she had done. But while his absence had given Felicia an early night, she had spent it sulking.

This morning Kedah had been off looking at

potential hotel sites, and she had sat in bed on the phone, liaising with his flight crew for their trip to Zazinia tomorrow.

Now she was meeting him for lunch, to go through the agenda for his trip home. There the artist would be able to work on his portrait, and there his father would discuss a wedding with his son.

That *had* to be the issue, Felicia decided. She was quite sure that Kedah had no desire to marry.

The restaurant she had chosen was dark and cool, and uninviting enough to keep the less than extremely well-heeled away.

'I have a booking,' she said. 'Felicia Hamilton.'

'Of course.'

When she had booked the restaurant Felicia had told them she was meeting an important guest and would like their very best table. She hadn't told them just how important her guest was, though.

It was a little game she played, and she smiled as she was led through the stunning restaurant to a gorgeous low table.

Indeed, it *was* beautiful.

There were plump cushions on the floor and the table was dressed with pale orchids. As she lowered herself onto a cushion she could hear the couple behind her laughing and chatting as she set up her work station.

She took a drink of iced water as she waited for Kedah to arrive, and again tried to fathom what trouble his wedding could pose.

There might be a baby Kedah? Felicia pondered. A pregnant ex, perhaps?

But, no, she was quite sure that Kedah would handle that in his own matter-of-fact way.

What about a pregnant prostitute?

That would surely rock the palace and destroy any chance for Kedah to remain as Crown Prince. Though she couldn't really imagine Kedah having to *pay* for sex—or even caring what others thought if he chose to do so.

Felicia took another long sip of iced water. She tended to do that when she thought of Kedah in that way—and she thought of Kedah in that way an awful lot...

Despite her very strict 'Never mix business with pleasure' motto, Felicia occasionally indulged in a little flirt with him—or rather, a very intense flirt. And there were odd moments when she felt as if her clothes had just fallen off. He made her feel naked with his eyes, although he was always terribly polite.

Felicia knew she'd have trouble saying no if he so much as crooked a finger in her direction. He hadn't, though—which was just as well, because he'd be in for a rude shock. There was no way Felicia would turn into one of those simpering *Your pleasure is all mine, Kedah* women he had a very frequent yen for.

Sweet.

That was the type of women he chose—or rather that was how they appeared until they were dumped.

Then it was Felicia who dealt with their angry, tearful outbursts.

She had almost been able to picture Beth, the actress, kicking her neighbour's blind cat when she'd told her that Kedah would not be taking her calls anymore.

'Have you thought about a gift?' Felicia had asked her, while trying to keep a straight face.

Yes, she had found out on her third day of working for Kedah that his aggrieved exes were sent a brochure from which to choose a gift.

No diamonds or pearls from Kedah—jewellery was too personal, of course. But a luxury holiday brochure was theirs to peruse. After all, what better than a week in the South of France or a trip to Mustique to help soothe that wounded heart? The only downside was that Sheikh Kedah would not be there.

He had already moved on to the next.

Beth had chosen to take her broken heart for a little cruise around the Caribbean. Felicia might have told her she'd have stood far more chance of a repeat night with Kedah if she'd told Felicia to pass on to him precisely what he could do with his brochure.

No one ever did.

But, while Kedah seemed at ease with his wretched reputation, there *had* to be more to why he wanted her nearby than to introduce her to the managers of all his hotels around the globe.

Why did Felicia need to know that the Dubai hotel

manager was an anxious sort but a wonderful leader? Why had he taken great pains to have her meet his accounts managers and his team of lawyers?

It just didn't make sense.

She looked up because, from the rustling and whispers amongst the patrons, it would seem that someone stunning had just arrived—and of course there he was.

She had recovered from the faint-inducing sight of Kedah in a suit, but here in Dubai he wore traditional attire and each day was a delicious surprise to the senses. On this fine day the angels had chosen for him a robe in cool, completely non-virginal white, and such was his beauty and presence that he turned every head as he made his way over.

His *keffiyeh* was of white-on-white jacquard, with knotted edges, and was seemingly casually tied. He was unshaven, but very neatly so. His lips were thick and sexy, the cupid's bow at the top so perfect one might be forgiven for thinking it tattooed. But this was all natural. Felicia had inspected that mouth closely enough to be very sure of that.

He looked royal and haughty and utterly beautiful, from his expensive cool head right down to his sexy leather-clad feet. Then his eyes lit on her, and the beautiful mouth relaxed into a warm smile—one that didn't just light up his features, but his whole being.

Auras were supposed to be indistinguishable,

even non-existent, yet Kedah wore his golden glow like a heavy fur coat.

He was a wolf in prince's clothing. Felicia knew that.

Such delectable clothing, though!

And *such* a stunning man...

Of course it wasn't only the women who noted his suave arrival—inevitably the head waiter came dashing over, clearly troubled at the inadequate seating arrangements for such an esteemed guest.

'You didn't say that you were dining with Sheikh Kedah,' he admonished her.

'I *did* say I was meeting an important guest,' Felicia said sweetly.

'Then please accept our sincere apologies. We have given you the wrong table—it is our mistake. Allow me...' He was gathering up her phone, her tablet, the whole mini-office that she set up whenever she met with Kedah.

'Of course.'

Felicia smiled to herself as she was bundled over to a stunning table—one where there was no chance of hearing their neighbours' conversation. The only sound was the gentle cascade of a fountain, the view of the marina was idyllic, and here the floor was entirely theirs.

'You played your game again,' he commented as they sat down opposite the other.

'I did.' Felicia nodded, and then met and held his gaze.

His eyes were thickly lashed, and he had a way of looking at her that honestly felt as if she were the only person present on the planet. He gave his absolute full attention in a way that was unlike anybody Felicia had ever known.

'Why don't you just say in the first place that you are meeting me?' he asked, because this happened rather a lot when Felicia booked their meetings.

'Because I like watching them fluster when you arrive.'

Kedah would like to see Felicia fluster—and yet she was always measured and poised and gave away so little of herself.

He would like to know more.

The thought continually surprised him. Kedah did not get involved with staff, yet over the past few weeks he had found himself wondering more and more about Felicia and what went on in her head.

It was a pretty head—one that was usually framed with shoulder-length hair. But today her hair was worn up. It was too severe on her, Kedah thought. Or was it that she'd lost a little weight? And he could see that she'd put on some make-up in an attempt to hide the smudges under her eyes.

Gorgeous eyes, Kedah thought. They regularly changed shade. Today they were an inviting sea-green, but he would not be diving in.

He did not want to muddy things—he needed her on board and, given that his relationships ran to days rather than weeks, he did not want to risk losing her over something as basic and readily available as sex.

Yet all too often they tipped into flirting. Kedah usually didn't bother—there was little need for it when you were as good-looking and as powerful as he. Yet he enjoyed their conversations that turned a seductive corner on occasion. Though Felicia had promised him discretion, there were times when he wanted her naked in bed beside him. He wanted to laugh as she told him tales about her former bosses.

Or 'clients', as Felicia referred to them.

That irked him.

He had seen her list of references, and some of the names there had had his jaw gritting. And, yes— he'd wondered all too often how close Felicia might have been to them. That was another thing that irritated him, but it would hardly be fair to question her about it.

He remembered now that he was cross with her for last night.

'Felicia, when I ask you to make a theatre booking for my date and myself, please do better in future.'

She knew he was referring to the previous night. At five, he had suddenly decided he wanted two of the hottest tickets in town.

'I got you the best available seats,' Felicia said. 'And I had to call in a favour to secure them.'

'Again...' he sighed '...you declined to say for whom you were booking.'

'You told me at my interview that you expect discretion.'

'I *expect* the best seats,' Kedah said. 'Had they not recognised me, I'd have been stuck behind a pillar. When you ring to make any booking in future, you are to tell them that it is for me.'

'That will ruin my game.'

'Tough,' he said. 'Right, let's go through my schedule. I want you to arrange some time for me to go to the States in a couple of weeks.'

And as she stared at him a thought suddenly occurred to her. Maybe he was already married—maybe that was the scandal that was about to hit.

'Do you go to America a lot?' she asked.

He nodded.

'Where?'

'All over. Though mainly New York. My friend Matteo lives there.'

'The one with the motor racing team?'

Kedah nodded.

Wild Matteo, who was known for his penchant for gambling and high-octane living.

'Have you ever been to Vegas?' she asked him.

'Felicia…' Kedah sighed again. 'Where is this leading?'

'I just wondered if you'd been to Vegas with Matteo…' She gave him a smile. 'And perhaps done something there that you might regret?'

'I don't waste time with regrets,' he said. 'And

I don't like wasting time—which we are. Let's go through tomorrow's agenda.'

They were saved from that, though, as the waiter somewhat nervously approached with mint tea. As Kedah looked up she felt the shifting of his attention. He was polite and engaged with the waiter, and as they spoke in Arabic she watched as he put the young man at ease.

He was arrogant, and yet he was kind.

Arrogant in that he expected the best and most often got it.

But then he could also be very kind.

'What would you like to eat?' Kedah asked Felicia.

'Fruit,' Felicia said. 'Something light.'

'Sounds good.'

He ordered, and when they were alone again he asked her how she was finding the hotel. Given he had not just designed the hotel but owned it, Felicia knew this was no idle enquiry.

'It's amazing,' she told him. 'Though I'd love to have some time to actually enjoy the facilities.'

Instead rather a lot of her time had been spent driving around to meet with the staff at his other acquisitions, or standing in the blistering sun scouring potential sites for Kedah to build on.

'I think I've found the site for its brother,' Kedah told her.

'Do buildings have a gender?'

'Mine do.'

'From conception?' Felicia asked. 'Do you decide

before you start the design that this one is going to be a boy?'

He smiled, and for Felicia the rays were as golden as the sun outside as he pondered her question.

'I guess I do,' he said. 'I want to go and have another look at the site after lunch, and then meet with a surveyor. You'll need sensible shoes.'

Joy!

Their lunch was served—citrus fruit and dragon fruits and sweet plump figs, as well as a light lemongrass mousse that just melted on her tongue. As they ate he asked her more questions about the hotel and she answered honestly.

Most of the time he liked it that she did—he was terribly used to his staff pandering to him. Her opinion was always refreshing, as well as at times rather blunt.

Kedah was, of course, up in the royal suite at the hotel, where every detail was taken care of and his every whim predicted. He wanted to know what it was like for a Western businesswoman traveller, so she was slumming it on the luxurious twenty-fourth floor with her own lap pool and butler.

'It's gorgeous.'

'Tell me what I don't know.'

Felicia thought hard. It really was difficult to be critical about somewhere so divine, but she pondered his question for a moment and was finally able to find a tiny fault. 'I think the service is a bit inconsistent.'

He watched as she bit on a piece of dragon fruit and waited for her to elaborate.

She soon obliged.

'Like, last night there weren't any chocolates on my pillow.'

'Poor Felicia.'

'I'm just saying,' she told him. 'You come to expect these things. Now, if I'd *never* had chocolate on my pillow I wouldn't have missed it, but I really sulked last night when they forgot…'

Or had she sulked because Kedah had gone off, out to the theatre? She wasn't sure, but certainly chocolate would have helped if that had been the case.

'First world problem.' She smiled.

'Noted,' Kedah said. 'If you came back to Dubai would you choose to stay there again?'

He was rather taken aback when she immediately shook her head.

'I don't think so.'

'Why?'

'I like trying new things.'

'If you're satisfied there should be no need or inclination to try anything else. I want to know why you wouldn't return.'

'Well, it's stunning, but…' She let out a breath and then decided she should perhaps check before being completely frank. 'Kedah, do you *really* want me to criticise one of your babies?'

I dare you to, his eyes told her. 'Go on,' he said politely.

'Well, as nice as it all is, I find it to be a bit impersonal,' Felicia responded, and she watched his tongue roll into his cheek. 'You *did* ask.'

'I did.'

'It just needs those extra touches,' Felicia offered.

'Such as…?'

'I don't know.' She shrugged. 'Maybe coloured towels, or something. I'm sick of white.'

She was—for she looked at his robe and she wanted it gone. She looked down to her hands and wanted them to be suddenly wrapped in his.

And *that* was the trouble with Kedah.

Not the terribly long hours, nor the jet lag, and it wasn't even the endless little black book she ran for him.

It was *this*.

These moments sitting with him.

These moments when flirting was a thought away…when she felt every conversation would be better executed in bed.

'You can do better than that,' he said.

Felicia had to drag her mind back to their conversation, actually force herself to remember they were discussing his hotel and not lean across the table and tell him that, yes, she *could* do far, far better.

'I don't have much experience in hospitality, remember?' she snapped wondering for possibly the millionth time what the hell he had hired her for.

Kedah could be boring!

Truly.

It was a terrible thing to admit but, just as when he had dimmed the lights and, instead of thrilling her, had proceeded to numb her brain with his hotel presentation, now—when they were in sumptuous surroundings and there was all this energy present—they sat discussing, of all things, towels.

He was driving her to distraction.

'The décor is black and brown in my American chain of hotels,' Kedah mused. 'The towels there are too.'

'Yum…' Felicia snarked.

'It actually works very well.'

'Why am I here, Kedah?' She was exhausted with not knowing. 'Why are we sitting here discussing bloody *towels*…?'

'Décor is important.'

'Then hire someone who cares!' she snapped. 'And tell me why I'm here.'

'You'll know when you need to.'

'Are you married?' The question tumbled out. 'Was there a drunken mistake that turned into a Mrs Kedah that I'm going to have to explain away?'

'Is that why you were asking about Vegas?'

He put his head back and laughed and she wanted her mouth on his throat.

'Felicia, I'm not married.'

'Is there a baby…?'

'You have too much imagination.'

'Er… Kedah, I don't think you and your lady-friends are merely holding hands. Accidents happen.'

'Not to me,' he said. 'I make sure of that.'

He honestly admired Felicia, because even as they discussed his strict use of birth control she didn't blush.

'However,' he mused, 'it wouldn't be a problem.'

'Your father would *welcome* the news?' Felicia asked, in a somewhat sarcastic tone, but it didn't faze him.

'It would be dealt with. I wouldn't be the first Crown Prince in our history to have a child out of wedlock. But Vadia would deal with that sort of thing—not you. Enough now,' he said, and went back to his schedule. 'We'll meet in the foyer at five tomorrow morning and get to Zazinia around mid-day,' he said. 'My time will be taken up with family stuff. There won't be much for you to do.'

'So why can't I just fly home?'

She was itching to get home—for a night in her flat without the alarm set for the crack of dawn the next morning. For a full twenty-four hours away from the burn of his eyes.

'Because…'

He couldn't answer straight away. Usually he *didn't* bring his London PA home with him. Occasionally he brought Anu, because she was from Zazinia, but there was absolutely no reason for bringing Felicia other than that he wanted her there.

'It's cheaper to have you there with me than to fly you home separately.'

'Oh, please!' She smiled sweetly.

'The Crown Prince's wing is being refurbished. I might need you...'

'To haul stone from the quarries?' she teased.

'To take some photos and jot down my suggestions.' He was stern. 'If it's not too much trouble?' She really was a terrible PA. 'As I said, I'll be busy with formal stuff. My portrait needs to be completed. Then there will be a dinner with my family.'

'That will be nice.'

Kedah gave her nothing—not a roll of the eyes, not even a small smile at her slightly sarcastic comment—but she knew there was trouble between the brothers.

'And then there's the matter of your wedding.'

'Yes.'

'And will you?' Felicia asked. 'Be taking a bride?'

'I might.' Kedah nodded.

He was tired of his father using his marital status as an excuse for things not to move along. Perhaps he would call his father's bluff and tell him to get things underway.

When he had said that he might be considering marriage, for the first time Felicia's expression faltered. She fought quickly to right it, but Felicia knew she'd been seen and so moved to cover it.

'I loathe weddings. I hope I shan't have to arrange that?'

'Don't worry.' He shook his head. 'The palace will take care of all that. You'll just be arranging a few final wild nights for me, leading up to it.'

'Look out, London.' Felicia rolled her eyes.

'Look out, world,' he corrected, for if he were to marry then he intended to use his last weeks of freedom unwisely. Except he hadn't been. Lately he hadn't. Last night it hadn't just been the seating arrangements that had got on his nerves.

It had been the company.

He had wanted Felicia beside him, and that might have been the reason he had dropped his date back to her hotel early.

'Then again,' Kedah said, 'if I am to choose a bride in a matter of weeks, perhaps it *is* time for me to be more discreet.'

She did not meet his gaze. Perhaps she had missed the opening, he thought, for she was signalling the waiter and asking for more water.

That was bold for here in Dubai. Usually only a male would signal the waiter, but then that was Felicia: bold.

Tough.

She was possibly the one woman who would *not* go losing her head if they were to sleep together.

'Felicia...' he said, and then, for once unsure how to broach things, he asked another question. 'Are you enjoying your work?'

'Not really,' she admitted. 'It's nothing like I expected. I thought I'd be putting out fires after big Kedah-created scandals.'

'How did you get into all that?'

She hesitated. Usually there was no way that Felicia would discuss her personal life, and yet if she wanted to know more about him maybe it was time to reveal something of herself. And he *was* good company.

Terribly so.

She might not be thrilled by her job description, but there was no doubt that she enjoyed being with him.

It was when she wasn't that her issues arose.

And so she found herself telling him a little. 'My father had a prominent job, but as far back as I can remember he got embroiled in scandal. Affairs, prostitutes…' Felicia coldly stated the facts. 'My mother and I were regularly schooled in what to say and what not to say. How to react…how to smile. Now I get paid to tell others the same.'

'Did your mother leave him in the end?' Kedah asked.

'No, after all he'd put her through it was my father who ended the marriage,' Felicia said. 'All the times she'd stood by him counted for nothing in the end. He planned how to leave her and did all he could to protect himself and his new girlfriend. The family home went—as did my boarding school. And I found out that my friends weren't really my friends. By the time he had dragged out the court proceedings I was well out of school. I left at sixteen and got a job in an office to support my mother.'

'Yet *you* are the PA everyone wants. Why?'

'My first boss. I never even saw him much, apart from setting up a meeting room. Anyway, scandal hit—as it often does—and the PR people he had working for him were seriously clueless. I knocked on his door and told him I could sort it for him.'

'How old were you?'

'I'd have been about nineteen,' Felicia said.

'He believed you?'

'He had no choice. He was up to his neck in scandal. I spoke to the press. I laughed at their inferences. I dealt with it just as I'd been taught to while I was growing up.'

'How is your mother now?'

Felicia didn't answer. She just gave a small shrug.

He sensed that she was finished talking about it. The subject moved back to work and there it remained, even after their meal had concluded.

Yet Kedah was curious.

'You'll need sensible shoes,' he reminded her as they walked to his car.

'Then you need to buy me some.'

She attempted humour, but she was still all churned up from thinking about her mother.

A little while later they stood on a man-made island and Kedah told her his vision for the hotel he was thinking of building there.

'What do you think?' he asked.

Usually he cared for no one else's opinion, yet he was starting to covet hers.

'It sounds a lot like the other one.'

It was possibly the most offensive thing she could have said, and yet her honesty made him smile.

'That's why I call them brothers.'

'Can't they just be siblings?' Felicia asked. 'Could this one not be a girl?'

He thought for a moment and, as terrible an assistant as she was, Felicia gave him pause.

Perhaps he *could* consider a gentler version of the other hotel. The Dubai skyline was ultra-modern, and there were some stunning architectural feats. From tall rigid towers to soft golden buildings in feminine curves. Perhaps it was time to try something different.

'See over there…?' He pointed. 'That was my first design. Well, along with Hussain.'

'Now, that's *definitely* a he!' Felicia said, because it was a huge phallic tower, rising into the sky.

'You're getting the idea.' Kedah smiled. 'It was my first serious project. Well, my second. I had designed a building for my home, but it was vetoed.'

'Is that a modified version of it?' Felicia asked.

'No. That design could never have worked here. There was a mural and…' He shook his head. 'I worked on this with Hussain. He is from my homeland, and studied architecture with my father, but *his* hands are tied there too…' Kedah halted.

'In what way?'

He thought for a moment and realised there was no harm in telling her, and as they chatted they walked away from the car and towards the water's edge.

'There are so many regulations back home. No window can overlook the royal beach…no building can be as high as the palace…'

'I'm sure you could work your way around them.'

They had toyed with each other and, yes, occasionally they had flirted, and of course Kedah had wondered what it would be like to know Felicia in the bedroom.

Now with one sentence she had changed things.

It was as if she had a little jewelled sword in her hand and had sliced straight through the chains that kept anybody from entering his heart.

She was the very first person who had not immediately derided his vision for his homeland.

Here was someone who did not instantly reject nor dismiss his ideas.

Even Hussain, to whom he had entrusted his visions, constantly told Kedah that he dreamed too big for his home.

'It's complicated, Felicia.'

'Life *is*.'

'We should get back,' he said, and he took her elbow to guide her back towards the car.

'What time are we meeting the surveyor?'

'Two,' Kedah said, and his voice was suddenly brusque. 'Though I won't need you there. Go back to the hotel and use some of the facilities.'

'You're giving me the afternoon off?' Felicia frowned. 'Why?'

'I *can* be nice.'

'I never said you couldn't.' She gave him a little nudge.

It was just that—a playful nudge. But Felicia did not play like that and neither did Kedah.

It was a tease—a touch that would have gone unnoticed had they been more familiar.

Yet they were *not* familiar.

They just happened to ache to be.

And so instead of walking they stood there, on an empty man-made island. His driver was some distance away, endlessly on his phone, and as the hot wind whipped at one of her loose curls Kedah resisted tucking it behind her ear.

'Will you tell me something, Felicia?'

'Maybe.'

'Do you flirt with *all* your clients?'

'I don't flirt.'

'I disagree.'

He was rather too direct.

'While I accept,' Kedah continued, 'that you don't tip up your face or bat your lashes—in fact you don't invoke any of the more usual tactics—you *do* flirt. And I just wondered if it was the same with all your...*clients*?'

She heard the implication. 'You make me sound like a whore.'

'Please forgive me for any offence caused—

absolutely none was meant. I am just curious as to what you are here for. I employed you as my PA and yet you don't seem to want that job.'

'I'm tired of the games, Kedah, and I'm tired that even after eight weeks you still don't trust me with the truth.'

'Okay—here it is. I believe the Accession Council will meet soon, and that there will be turbulent times ahead as my suitability for the role of Crown Prince is called into question.'

'I know all that,' Felicia said. 'So where do I fit in?'

'I need someone who knows the business—someone who, when it all kicks off—'

'Kicks off?' she checked.

'I believe my brother will have the backing of the elders. More troubling for me is that I believe my father may support him also. If that is the case I shall be forced to take it to the people to decide. That would cause a lot of unrest and bad publicity...'

'You'd want me to convince your people that just because you've run a bit wild...?' She paused as Kedah smiled—a lightly mocking smile.

'Felicia,' he said. 'My people *love* me.'

She didn't get it. She could not see where she might fit in to all this. 'They love you regardless?'

'No.' He shook his head. 'I would never expect them to support me regardless. They love me because of what I stand for, what I can do for them.'

'Oh.'

Kedah did not want to tell anyone—unless he was

forced to—that the scandal that was looming was not one of his making.

Correction.

Sometimes he *did* want to tell her.

Back in the restaurant, when Felicia had spoken of her father, he had wanted to share his own truth. But that was an unfamiliar route for Kedah and so still he'd held back.

He held back from revealing the full truth now.

'I am spending time in Zazinia. You can deal with the empire I have built and answer with ease the many questions that will be hurled.'

'That's it?' Felicia frowned. 'That's all you want me there for? To deal with the press? I don't believe you.'

That *had* been it.

Kedah had wanted someone tough and strong to take care of the press as he devoted his time to his country. He knew how bad things were likely to get if the elders and Mohammed called his parentage into question.

Never had he considered revealing that to another— especially not a lowly PA.

And he wasn't now.

Instead he was considering discussing it with Felicia—the woman who had held him entranced since she had stood outside his office eight weeks ago.

He was supposed to marry soon. He did not need her tearful and scorned. And yet with every minute that passed between them he felt as if they were falling slowly into bed, into sex, into want. She could deny it, yet he *felt* it. And if they were about to cave then he needed to know she could remain strong, that sex could be separated from the vital tasks ahead.

And possibly, Kedah pondered as she stared back at him, Felicia was the one person who would be able to do that.

It irked him that she considered him a *client*.

And it troubled him that she might have been involved with some of her clients in the past.

Then again, if he wanted the toughest of the tough perhaps it should not.

There was no polite way to ask.

'Your eyes were the shade of the sea at the restaurant. Now they are hooker green.'

Her breath tightened and she flashed him a look of fire.

'It's an actual shade,' he said. 'And you *are* flirting, Felicia. Your eyes invite me closer at times.'

'Perhaps I'm just responding in kind.'

'I want you,' he told her.

He just stated his case.

Her clothes felt as if they had disintegrated again. She felt as if she were standing there stark naked even though his eyes never left hers.

'I am thinking now that unless you go I shall cancel the surveyor and take you up to my suite…'

'And you presume that I'll join you? You just assume I want you too?'

Felicia tried—she really did. But had his driver got out and started clapping she'd have joined him. Because it was a joke that she didn't want Kedah. She was *so* turned on.

Click your fingers and I'll come turned on.

And he smiled that arrogant smile that told her he absolutely *knew* she would join him should he so choose.

'The thing is I need you working for me more than I need you between the sheets.' Right now that was debatable, but although Kedah regretted little, he knew that *this* he might. 'I don't want tears in the morning, and I want you to continue to work for me rather than moping about in Mustique, so I suggest that you go back to the hotel and have a think. I don't want you agreeing to something you might later regret.'

'You've got a nerve.'

'I know I have.'

'Kedah, I've booked for your date to be collected for you at ten tonight…'

'That gives you several hours to make up your mind. She can easily be cancelled.'

Oh, yes, if there was a scale of playboys then Kedah would definitely be at the extreme end.

In all her imaginings—and, yes, there had been plenty—they were talking one moment and then somehow had moved seamlessly to bed. Never had she thought she'd be so frankly propositioned. That Kedah would have her cancelling his date so he could slot *her* in.

Thankfully he'd just made it a whole lot easier to say no!

'I don't need several hours to make up my mind,' she answered. 'Enjoy your night.'

She turned her head as a car approached. It would seem that the surveyor was here.

'I'm going to enjoy my afternoon off.'

'Do.'

She didn't.

The lap pool was paid a visit, but it did not clear her head, and a lengthy massage, although divine, did little to relax her.

Dinner for one felt lonely that night.

But she made herself sit through it.

Ten p.m. came, and when it had safely passed she went up to his suite.

He was out.

Clearly Kedah waited for no one.

The maid was there, preparing the bed, and the butler helped her to pack up his things for their early-morning start.

She stared at the bed with a mixture of pride and regret.

Pride that she had not succumbed.

Regret that she would never know how it felt to be Kedah's lover.

She set his alarm for four and headed down to her own suite. As she opened the door, still cross— *so* cross with him for his suggestion—still he made her smile.

There were chocolates on her pillow.

Many, many chocolates on her pillow. All perfectly wrapped.

But more than that, as she walked into the bathroom to strip, she was met with a rainbow of colour.

Kedah wasn't boring, and even towels could be sexy, Felicia thought as she showered and then chose from the selection.

There were deep crimsons and burnt oranges— but she bypassed them and reached for another towel...one possibly the shade of hooker green.

She should be offended, and yet Kedah had removed that. From the day she had met him she had rightly guessed that he saved his issues for outside the bedroom. If sex was reduced to a business arrangement then so be it for him.

Could *she* do it, though?

Could she simply submit for the bliss of knowing what it was like to be made love to by him?

Kedah seemed to think it was doable. But then he assumed that she was tough and that he was simply another client.

Oh, no, he wasn't.

He was slowly stealing her heart.

What if she never revealed that?

Felicia had been trained to hide her true feelings from a very young age. This could possibly serve as the ultimate test.

Wrapped in her towel, she walked to the bed and peeled open a chocolate. As she tasted it, dark, sweet and silky on her tongue, she saw a note.

Handwritten by him.

Think about it.

She couldn't *stop* thinking about it—no matter how she tried.

CHAPTER FOUR

Where was he?

A pre-dawn Dubai sky offered no answers as Felicia peered out through the window of her hotel suite. There were yachts lit up on the marina. No doubt there were parties aplenty still happening, and if Kedah was running true to form he might well be down there amongst them.

His butler had just called her to say that there had been no response to his wake-up call.

'Can you go in and check?' Felicia had asked, but the butler had explained that because the 'Do Not Disturb' light was on he couldn't, even though it was doubtful Kedah was there.

Apparently the Sheikh had returned to the hotel after midnight, but had been seen heading out again around two a.m.

When Felicia tried his cell phone it was off.

He was *always* on time, Felicia told herself as she headed into the bathroom and checked her appearance. She would have to change on the plane, as Kedah had told her the dress code was strict in Zazinia, but for now she was wearing a navy shift dress. Before heading out she would add to it a small short-sleeved bolero to cover her arms.

Felicia really needed her concealer this morning, after a night spent pondering their conversation, but she decided to do her make-up on the plane too.

Right now she was too busy ruing the hours she had spent considering getting further involved with Kedah if his reaction was simply to stay out all night.

Hell, yes, she was angry.

She had worked with him for eight weeks and the last four had been spent travelling.

Soon they would be back in London and a safer distance would be easier to maintain.

To think she might have succumbed at the last hurdle!

She wasn't just cross with Kedah, she was angry with herself as she marched out of her bathroom. She went to put up her hair, but simply didn't have the upper arm strength or the concentration this morning.

Another thing that could wait for the plane.

There was a knock on the door to her suite, and she opened it to the bellboy who had come to collect her luggage.

'Has Sheikh Kedah's luggage been taken down?' Felicia checked.

'Not yet,' the bellboy informed her. 'We cannot go in if the "Do Not Disturb" light is on.'

'Even if he's probably not there?'

'Even then.'

Felicia let out a tense breath as the door closed and she was again left alone with some choices to make.

She had access to his suite—of course she did. Last night she and the butler had packed his belongings there, leaving the necessaries out for the morning.

All Kedah had had to do was tumble into bed with the requisite blonde and then get up on time.

She headed out to the elevators, but instead of going down to the foyer, where they had arranged to meet, she used her security pass and pressed the button for the royal floor.

A rather worried butler greeted her.

'The "Do Not Disturb" light is still on. I really cannot go in.'

'Well, *I* can.'

The butler was slightly startled at her assertive tone, but she took out the swipe card for the room, gave the door several sharp knocks and then entered.

Please, she begged silently, *if he's in here then let him be alone.*

The suite was in darkness. There was the sound of running water and she wondered if he had fallen asleep in the sunken bath. The sound came from the pool, she realised as she saw the drapes gently billowing in the breeze and realised that the huge glass doors were open.

She walked silently over the thick carpet and out to the stunning alfresco area. It truly was an oasis. High in the sky, there was a colourful garden and a large pool that jutted out over the ocean.

It made her dizzy even to think of it, though Kedah told her he swam in it each day.

Felicia walked over. No, he was *not* practising the breaststroke.

She stepped back from the edge as the warm morning air dusted her cheeks and blew at her hair.

There weren't any signs of a wild party, though he must have been out here at some point for the doors to be open.

It really was beautiful, Felicia thought. So much so that for a moment she forget her mission to find the missing Sheikh and simply took in the stunning view.

The navy sky was fading and was now dressed in ribbons of silver and various shades of blue as the sun prepared to break into the horizon. Ahead, Felicia could see the island where they had stood yesterday and spoken.

She could stand and bristle with indignation, or she could wrap her arms around herself and try to hold on to the shiver within her that Kedah evoked.

He moved her.

Just that.

He took feelings and memories that were usually guarded and shook them. He jolted awake desires and emotions so that she was standing there feeling as if she was on the top of the world and convincing herself that she could handle it.

That a night or two would surely be worth it, just to have known that bliss.

And there was always the brochure. Yes, she would mope, but only for a week, and then she would circle Mustique and spend time there rehabilitating her heart.

No.

She could *not* sleep with him and then continue to work for him; she could *not* pretend it didn't matter when he discarded her and moved on to the next woman.

And there was no way she would be a filler between drinks.

She actually laughed at the nerve of him.

'Is everything all right, madam?'

Felicia turned and saw the butler, hovering in the doorway.

'Everything's fine.' She nodded. 'I'll just check to see if he's asleep.'

She headed back inside and with mounting trepidation walked towards the main bedroom in the suite. The double doors were closed and she glanced at the butler, who gave a worried shake of his head as she went to knock. He was certain that their most esteemed guest should not be disturbed.

'He might be unwell,' Felicia offered. She didn't think it for a moment, but it was the excuse she would give to Kedah if he called her out for disturbing him.

'Kedah!' Felicia knocked loudly. 'Kedah, the plane's scheduled to leave...'

When there was no response she opened the door. Relief.

She wasn't disturbing an intimate moment.

He was not there, and yet she could see that he had been—the bed was rumpled and unmade and there were several thick white towels dropped on the floor. And his visit had been a recent one, for the musky, woody scent of his cologne lingered.

Perhaps he had come back from the party and showered and changed before heading out again?

Bedded his date, showered and changed, Felicia thought with a gnawing unease as she closed the door.

She was tired of playing detective, tired of putting the pieces together on his depraved life.

Tired of it all, really.

Especially saying no.

'I'll just pack up the last of his things,' Felicia said to the butler as she turned off the alarm.

She headed to the wardrobe and took out the case she had left. There wasn't much to pack. Most of it had been done last night, and once the bellboy had come to collect his luggage she headed back down to the foyer.

His vehicle was waiting, the engine purring, and his driver was—as always—on the phone. Felicia was grateful that the doorman didn't attempt small talk. Instead he handed Felicia her preferred brew in a takeaway cup and she said her thanks and took a grateful sip.

Dawn was breaking and Dubai was now pretty in pink. And then, as transfixing as the sunrise, Kedah appeared, walking slowly as if there was no King or country awaiting his imminent arrival, no jet on the runway ready and primed to carry him there.

She would have loved to say, *Look what the cat dragged in*—but, as always, he was immaculate. In fact he looked as if he were just leaving for the night rather than arriving back at dawn. He was a sight for Felicia's sleep-deprived eyes.

'Good morning,' he greeted her.

'You're late,' Felicia responded.

'So?' His response was surly and brief, and he glanced down at the coffee she held in her hand and then back up to her eyes. 'May I?'

Felicia handed him her coffee and he drained it, but then pulled a face. 'Too sweet.'

'It didn't stop you, though.'

Actually, last night it had.

Last night his mind had been on Felicia—so much so that he'd dropped his pouting date back at her hotel and returned to his room. Sleep had proved elusive, and a shower had done nothing to temper the urge to call Felicia and summon her to his suite.

The trouble was, he had known she was the one woman who might not take too kindly to his summons, and so instead he had headed onto the balcony and told himself to forget about her—at least for now. There was his trip home to get through first.

Zazinia had to be his priority—though he wasn't looking forward to this visit in the least. He knew there would be a confrontation with his father, and that there would be a push towards him choosing a bride.

Last night he had hoped to take his mind off his problems in the usual way, but he hadn't been able to.

Now the reason that he hadn't smiled back at him.

This morning her hair was worn down, though it was more wavy and unkempt than usual. She didn't wear a lot of make-up, but she had on none today.

She belonged on his pillow.

'Are you ready?' she asked him.

'Am I?' he asked. 'Did you finish my packing?'

'Yes,' she said. 'I went into your suite with the butler this morning. He didn't want to—he was worried we might disturb something.'

'There was nothing to disturb last night,' Kedah said. 'In fact there hasn't been anything to disturb for quite some time.'

'I don't believe you for a moment.'

'That's up to you. My theatre date bored me, as did my date last night. Did you get the chocolates?'

'You know I did.'

'Did you like the towels?' he asked. 'Oh, I apologise—I forgot there are things that bore you to discuss.'

She said nothing.

'Did you get my note?'

She nodded.

'And *did* you?' he asked.

And then he looked at the shadows under her eyes that were so much darker than before and the slight gritting of her jaw. The answer as to whether she had thought about it was clear.

'Of course you did.'

She wished she could go back to their first meeting, when she had been sure about never sleeping with him.

But she hadn't really been sure even then.

On sight she had wanted him, and that feeling remained.

'I'm going to freshen up,' Kedah said.

When he had left she stood there, as the driver made small talk and worried about angering Kedah's father, the King.

She remembered the tingle at the base of her spine at the way he said her name.

She did not mix business with pleasure, but he blurred all the lines.

He wanted the tough woman who had stepped into his office—which she still was—and yet Felicia was also aware that she liked him more than she should for such a relationship to work.

He didn't need to know that.

More than anyone, Felicia knew how to hold onto her heart.

'How long did he say?' the driver asked now. 'Apparently they're furious at the palace that he's so late. The captain's trying to sort out a flight path to make up the time…'

'He shouldn't be too long,' Felicia replied. 'I'll just go and see.'

She should text him, really.

It would be far safer.

Instead, just a few moments later, she stood at the door of his hotel suite.

She had the access card—of course she did—but usually if he was in there she'd knock first.

This morning she didn't.

She stepped into the entrance hall and saw Kedah was emptying his safe.

'You forgot my diamond.'

'Sorry.'

'Attention to detail, Felicia,' he said, and wagged his finger in a small scold.

'I told you on the first day that I would not make a good PA.'

'You did.'

He closed the safe and pocketed the stone, but made no move to walk towards her.

'You need to hurry up.'

His eyes met hers. 'Says who?'

'Word from the palace is that the King is concerned you haven't left yet. The pilot is going to try to make up the time…' All this was said as he walked towards her, and her voice was breathless.

'Oh, well.' He shrugged.

And now he stood right in front of her, and Felicia looked at his mouth and wondered what the rest of her life would feel like should she never taste it.

'Did you think about it?'

'Yes.'

It was pointless to lie, and the fact that she stood there rather than stepped back, that she met his beautiful gaze, spoke of the decision she had come to.

'We have to continue to work together,' he warned her.

'I know that. So there are things we need to discuss…' Felicia attempted, because she *would* be laying a few ground rules.

'There's no time for that now,' that beautiful mouth said. 'We can speak on the plane.'

But that was a full twenty-six minutes away, at best. And she looked at the dark pink of his lips and then the black roughness of his jaw. It would be cruel to look back on this moment and regret walking away.

And so she did not turn to go.

Instead she stood as his hand moved to her shoulder and he peeled away the strap of her bag. He placed the bag on an occasional table, and that gesture alone told her of the thoroughness of the kiss to come.

She was shaking—not outwardly, but there was a low tremble that seemed to start at midthigh and inch with every heartbeat nearer to her throat.

'Kedah,' Felicia warned again, 'we have to speak.'

'First we taste.'

There was no time for this. Kedah knew that. His father's mood would not be improved by his late arrival, and things were already tense.

And yet he too could not resist.

White-hot, Felicia turned him on. There had been a slow burn as he'd walked towards her. Now he was hard and ready, and he hadn't even tasted her mouth.

Now he did.

Their flesh, their tongues, finally met, and both were wet and wanting, and both moaned in mutual bliss as eight weeks of want found an outlet.

Their mouths moved slowly and appreciatively at first, relishing the heady taste that they made.

'That,' said Kedah, peeling his lips back just a little, 'was how I wanted to greet you on the first day.'

And there was something terribly freeing about it being a work deal, for she could be as provocative as all hell without being accused of being a tease.

'This,' she said, 'is how I wanted to greet *you*.'

She kissed him harder still, and Kedah loved it that she did not hold back from revealing her pleasure.

Her body was lithe, and it pressed into his as their tongues met. Provocatively, he ran a hand down her spine until it came to rest on one heart-shaped buttock while the other hand went to the back of her head so that he could kiss her more thoroughly.

It was more of a kiss than she had ever known.

She had a brief wish that their clothes would evap-

orate, because she knew herself that in that space of
time when he removed her clothes common sense
would kick in.

And she knew Kedah and where a kiss would
lead.

She pulled her face away, and her mouth was wet
and swollen, her skin pink and inflamed from the
roughness of his jaw.

He was hard against her, and her breasts were
aching for his touch, for his mouth, for any contact
he cared to bestow.

He kissed her again, but this time his fingers
tightened in her hair, and it was the roughest, most
thorough kissing of her life.

He held her hips and rubbed her against himself.

She peeled her mouth away and still he held her.
He could feel her body trembling as she fought the
writhing want within. Her eyes were green and her
mouth was open, dragging in air, and he held her
hair taut in his hand and fought not to tug it—hard.
He fought not to pull back her head and lower his
mouth again.

He stroked her where his hand cupped her bottom, and then he pulled her further in so she could
feel every generous inch of his hard length against
her stomach.

And it was too late to worry about the time, for
her fingers had moved to the row of small buttons
on his shirt and she'd exposed his muscular chest.

Kedah loved the way her hands were not shy—

how, as her mouth still merged with his, she toyed with his flat nipples and then, bored with them, let her hand creep down to the soft snake of silken hair that had entranced her from that first glimpse.

From her bag on the table her phone bleeped with a text message, just as the head of his erection nudged her palm.

'That will be the driver, telling me to hurry you up.'

'Hurry me up, then.'

And he felt her smile, for her lips stretched beneath his as he took her hand and ran it the length of his long, hard shaft.

His other hand pressed at her head, and she knew—because this was the kind of man she was choosing to get involved with—that from the direction of the pressure Kedah exerted she should be dropping to her knees—oh, right about *now*.

But he was in for that shock. For she had needs of her own and it would never be all about *him*.

'Kedah,' she said, and removed her hand as she lifted her head. 'We really don't have time for foreplay.'

She watched his eyes flare as she stepped back from his embrace and reached for her bag.

'Foreplay?' he checked.

'It's when—'

'I *do* know what it is, thank you,' he snapped.

'Good.' She smirked. 'I've got news for you, Kedah. I didn't come up here just to satisfy your needs. I have terms and conditions of my own!'

And she was doing it.

Somehow, against this very powerful man, she was holding her own.

'We need to get a move on, Kedah. I'll see you down there.'

CHAPTER FIVE

SIX FOOT THREE of sulking Sheikh boarded the plane.

Kedah did *not* need the complication of Felicia.

But he had tasted her now.

And *she* did not need the arrogance of him.

She wanted him, though.

They sat on his private jet and her skin was prickling—so much so that she almost went through her bag for antihistamines, till she realised this was no allergic reaction. She was on fire for *him*.

The take-off was smooth and he glanced up as a flight attendant came over.

'Can I get you anything, Your Highness?'

'Shaii.' Kedah asked for tea, and it was served in a long crystal glass and cold, as he liked it. It was refreshing and sweet but not soothing.

He took out the diamond that he carried and tapped it on the gleaming table. He saw Felicia glance over.

'That's a pretty elaborate worry bead.'

'I told you,' a surly Kedah replied. 'I never worry.'

The tapping resumed as he pulled up a file.

Not any old file.

He had been working on this for years, for it was Zazinia as he envisaged it.

Every plan he had submitted had been rejected, every vision he'd had for his home discounted, and they were all compiled in this one stunning display. He sat there watching as buildings rose before his eyes and bridges connected them. He had designed all the infrastructure—the roads and railways were splendidly linked—and yet none of it had been implemented. At every turn he had been thwarted. This was the reason Kedah was rarely home.

He closed the file and worked instead on a skyline that he *could* change. He started on some preliminary designs for his latest Dubai project.

He was considering linking the hotels—either with a monorail or possibly a tunnel. It would be a huge venture. Yet Felicia was right. Why link two hotels that were basically the same? Now, thanks to her, the gender was no longer clear, for he was thinking of a more recreational facility. One families or couples might choose to visit.

His plane was usually a second office, but she was invading his headspace. She was even influencing his hotel's design. So he closed the file. Hussain could work on it further, or tell him outright if he was dreaming too big, Kedah decided.

He opened his email and flicked over to Felicia

the files he wanted her to tidy up. He added a message telling her that he wanted her to write a cover note for Hussain, but then, distracted, realised he'd sent the wrong file.

For the first time since leaving the hotel he spoke to her.

'Delete the last email I sent,' Kedah said. 'The information I want you to forward to Hussain is in the one I am sending now.'

Always he could separate work and pleasure.

Not today.

He looked over to her and saw that the dress she was wearing was modest, but it would not be suitable for his home.

'Felicia?'

'Yes?'

'Did I tell you about the dress code in Zazinia?'

'You did.' She nodded. 'I'll change closer to when we land.' She turned and rather pointedly looked out of the window rather than prolonging their conversation.

'I'm going for a rest,' he told her. Normally Kedah just stalked off and it was left to Felicia to guess where he'd gone.

She turned and their eyes met as he stood and headed to the bedroom. He halted when he got to the door.

'There are three more hours' flying time,' he said. 'Is that sufficient for you?'

He walked into the bedroom and Felicia went into

her bag and took out a book. But the words all ran into each other and after a few minutes of pretending she put the book down.

There were moments in life from which you knew there would be no coming back.

If she entered his suite it would be one of those moments, she knew, for his kiss had offered her more than a glimpse of what it would be like to be with him.

He assumed she had slept with previous clients because she had let him assume that.

And she was lying to herself now, Felicia knew, by telling herself she could handle this.

Yet she had to.

He came with a warning, and he had stated the same.

This would end—and no doubt at a time of *his* choosing.

She sat for a moment and accepted that fact.

Desire won.

And yet she did have rules.

She wanted to be behind that door, wanted her time with him, and so she stood and headed to the bedroom.

She didn't knock. Instead she walked in. And there on the bed lay Kedah as she had never seen him before.

He had a sheet covering his lower half, but she knew that he was naked beneath the sheet. For now she just stood and stared at him and took in his beauty.

His chest was toned and there was a smattering of dark hair across it. His nipples were a deep shade of red and he was utterly exquisite. She followed the dark trail down, and through the sheet she could see the thick length of him against his thigh. The thought of him inside her was intensely thrilling.

'Undress,' he told her, and his voice had a rasp of impatience for she had kept him waiting again.

'Not yet,' she said, and then she stated her case. 'Kedah, as long as we last, there's only me...'

He just stared.

'If you see someone else, don't expect me back in your bed.'

'I shan't.'

His response was surprising. She had expected debate, or for him to state that he would do as he pleased.

'I have no interest in others...' He didn't. He hadn't in a while. 'I do have to marry, though.'

'I know you do.'

'So how about a long fling before that...?'

It was what she wanted—more than she had expected—and yet a warning sounded in her head, because it was already more than sex for her, and a prolonged affair with Kedah could only hurt more in the end.

'A fidelity trial?' he said.

She wanted his kiss. She wanted him to stand and kiss her to oblivion as he undressed her with skilled ease. Yet he did not.

'Take off your shoes,' he told her, and she stood there for a few seconds before doing so. 'Now undo your buttons…'

'I do know how to undress myself,' she snapped. Her voice was tense, and her head felt as if she had stepped off a merry-go-round.

He was nothing like any lover she had known, and that secretly thrilled her.

'Undo the buttons,' he said, but with less patience this time.

Her hands were shaking as she undid the row of buttons at the side of her dress, and the tension in the air made her almost dizzy.

She recalled that tone now. It was the same one he had used on the day they had first met, when he had told her to sit back down and that he hadn't finished with her yet. The effect was the same, and yet multiplied a thousandfold.

'Take it off over your head.'

'It doesn't come off that way.'

And instead she peeled it down the arms and her dress slid to the floor. She stood there, cross with herself for doing as she was told, yet angrily awaiting further instruction.

'Nice bra,' Kedah said. 'Now, take it off.'

'You.'

He flashed her a look as he moved to stand and she took in a long breath. It was the kind of breath she might take in private, before making a difficult phone call. The kind of breath she might take before opening the door to a stranger.

Yet it was the right kind of breath to take before a lean, toned body rose from the bed and the sheet fell away, to reveal him aroused and hard and walking towards hers.

'Turn around,' he said.

She resisted, but only in the hope that he would touch her, for her skin was screaming for contact, yet contact he refused to give.

'Turn around,' he said again, and this time she did as she was told. 'Now, undo your bra…'

'You can do it.'

'Don't annoy me any more than you already have.'

'Why?'

His mouth came close to the back of her head and his low voice in her ear made her want to arch her neck, to turn to kiss him, but she stood staring ahead.

'For insinuating, back at the hotel, that I would have left you unsatisfied.'

She turned her head then, and found him smiling. And he smiled as only Kedah could. He smiled as he had when he'd walked into that restaurant and seen her sitting there waiting for him. He smiled as he did when he greeted her each morning.

Yet it was different today, for there was no mistaking the deep intimacy levelled at her. There was absolute seduction in his eyes, and Felicia knew that if all that was left was this—if the plane fell from the sky right now—she was glad for this moment.

Game over. For it was Felicia who turned and smiled and wrapped her arms around his neck. They were back to deep kissing as he removed her bra—easily. His fingers stroked her breasts with feather-light strokes alternated with pinches that made her gasp in shocked pleasure.

Now, the solid nudge of his body was guiding her to the bed, and though she wanted to be there so badly still she wanted to stand for just a moment and fully savour the feel of him naked against her. He felt like silk beneath her fingers, and there was a wall of muscle that warned of pleasures to come. His mouth was firm and his tongue expert as his hands roamed her, strumming her rib cage or toying with her hip as he enjoyed the body he had been resisting for what felt like far too long.

She could feel the mattress pressing into the back of her thigh and fought to stay standing against him. Yet like a domino he toppled her onto the bed.

It was Kedah who remained standing, and she felt the scorch of his eyes as they roamed her flushed skin.

'Let's get rid of these,' he said.

He placed her feet on his thigh and she lifted her bottom to allow him to peel off her knickers as if he was opening the most delicate gift. Down her thighs he slid them, with such a lack of haste that she let out a moan—an absolute whimper.

His shaft jerked in response to it as Kedah discovered that the sound of Felicia moaning was a sound he craved.

She was always so brittle, so contained, it was a pleasure to hear her unravel.

Past her knees came the knickers, and then he ripped them down the final stage. Now she was naked, and soon she'd be his.

He knelt between her legs and Felicia had never known such absolute scrutiny. It felt as if he were kissing her all over, yet only his eyes caressed her for now.

'Turn over,' he told her, and she rolled to her front.

She rested her head on her forearm and waited—for whatever he so chose. Anticipation thrummed as she heard his ragged breathing, and then he placed a wet kiss right at the base of her spine.

'Kedah...'

His tongue was hot and slow and it moved in long circles. Her free hand moved to touch herself at such bliss but he caught her wrist.

It was an attack of the senses. Because now he parted her thighs and slipped his long fingers into her as his mouth worked the length of her spine.

She lifted her hair, just so that he might have access to her skin, and did not know if it was the bruising kiss to her neck or the stretch of his fingers inside her that caused her to make a low choking noise.

'Please...' she said, not knowing how to say that she wanted—no, *needed* more and more of this.

But he removed the pleasure and rolled her onto

her back. He opened her legs and moved so that he knelt between her knees. He wanted to take her there and then, and reached over the bedside for a condom, but the sight of her pink and glistening beckoned him for just a brief taste.

Felicia swore as he parted her lips and, instead of devouring her, licked her with just with the tip of his tongue. 'Don't...' she said, and her hands knotted into his hair as he teased her, scratched at her thighs with his jaw.

Kedah knew he was good, but he'd never enjoyed himself to this level. Hearing the panting in her voice and feeling the pressure of her thighs trapping him made him search deeper. Her sweet, musky taste was like nectar. Hot, she writhed, and his tongue devoured.

He was too slow, she decided, for she was suddenly frantic.

The sounds he made were low, and his possessive growl reverberated through her.

Her hands left his head and went to her own, tense fingers tightening in her hair as he raised her bottom.

He was relentless.

He should stop now, she thought as she started to come.

Please stop, she thought. Because she had never come so fully to a man's mouth—in fact she couldn't remember feeling like this *ever*.

She wanted to push him away, and yet she wanted for this never to end.

He felt the pulsing and the tension rise within her. And for Kedah there was a giddy triumph at hearing Felicia in the throes of the pleasure that he had procured for her. She made no logical sense as she pleaded for less while her body urged for more. And then it faded, and he felt her relax and grow calm, but this wasn't even close to being over.

He wanted his own release, and so he took her slowly, just kneeling up and pulling her in.

He toyed at her entrance and Felicia pushed herself up onto her elbows. She watched as he glanced over to the condoms scattered on the bed beside them, but they might as well have been in his office drawer back in London, for nothing must break the contact they made.

She told him that she was covered in ragged, breathless words. 'I'm on the pill...'

Both of them would usually have needed far more than that to continue. Felicia even let out a half-sob and a laugh at her own abandon. But both felt now that it was imperative not to lose the beauty of this moment.

They were on the edge of discovery, entering into uncharted water—and not just because of the lack of protection. It was the eye contact, the unbridled pleasure, and the care taken as he positioned her calves.

Kedah let out a moan as he slid into her oiled, tight warmth. His eyes came up to meet hers, but she was looking down at the blending of them.

'Felicia!'

He snapped her into eye contact with him, and she found there was nothing sexier than full-on looking into Kedah's eyes as he took her.

For a couple of moments that was exactly what he did. He moved to his whim along his thick length.

With anyone else she would have resisted, and yet he guided her so expertly and filled her so completely that all Felicia had to do was give in to the arm that held her up and lie back to receive the pleasure.

She felt the bliss of his weight and the reward of his kiss. His skin was immaculate as her hands slid down his loins and she knew that if she'd made a decision to do something rash then this was the right one.

He took her with force and passion and she returned the same—and almost a tussle ensued as they rolled so Felicia was on top.

'I want…' she said, but did not continue. She just wanted to come again, and there was such energy between them…such a mutual goal to give the other pleasure.

He had thought about what they might be like together and he had expected restraint, a tinge of regret too, and yet there was only fire and buried passion from Felicia.

'Slow down,' he said, and took her hips and jerked her down on his thick length over and over.

His hands moved up to her breasts and toyed with them, stretching her nipples as Felicia bit down on her lip. Then she leant forward to taste his salty skin as his hands roamed her buttocks.

He started thrusting upwards, and with that she had the pleasure of watching him release, and the sensation of the power of him within her.

She toppled forward, and as he came he slid her over and over down onto him, over the edge with him.

Their faces were next to each other and she could feel her hair was damp. Every part of her was more than warm, her skin was on fire, and she had never known anything like this feeling of silence and peace—this space they had walked into together.

He slipped her off him and she fell beside him, breathless, and looked him in the eye.

Then they smiled, because it had been better than they had hoped or dared to expect.

She wanted to touch and explore him, but they lay for just a moment, both thrumming in private bliss as they kissed each other down.

CHAPTER SIX

THEY LAY ENTWINED TOGETHER, and Kedah listened to the hum of the engines as the plane carried them to his home. Deeply sated, he found his mind was clearer.

Felicia's wasn't.

She lay with her head on his chest, listening to the steady thump of his heart as her hand toyed with the silky straight hair on his stomach that she had, right from the start, wanted to feel.

Now that she had, *still* she wanted.

'Can I ask you something?' Felicia spoke but, far too comfortable in his arms, did not raise her head.

'It depends what it is.'

Kedah was no open book.

'Do you want to be King?'

'Of course,' he answered as his hand stroked her bare arm. 'I was born to be King.'

'So why aren't you there all the time?'

'Because my plans to improve Zazinia are repeatedly turned down. I refuse to be an impotent Crown Prince...'

'I doubt there's any chance of that…' she said, and her hand crept down.

'I had a stand-off with my father and the old King some years ago,' Kedah told her. 'They had turned down every plan I had submitted and it was evident that they were never going to accept them. I asked for confirmation and they gave it to me—they did not welcome change. I love to design and so I chose to go it alone. That diamond I carry—it was from the sale of my first hotel. They loathe that I am self-made because it means that I am not beholden to them. I want, though, to make my land better for the people.'

'And now you can?'

'Perhaps.'

'The old King is dead,' Felicia pointed out.

'My father still chooses to listen to the elders and Mohammed.'

'I know you, Kedah—you could convince anyone of anything.' After all, she was in his bed. 'Your people love you.'

'I know they do.'

'What will happen when the Accession Council meet?'

'Mohammed shall state his case, and I shall state mine, and my father shall be asked to make a formal choice.'

'And if it isn't you, you'll take it to the people to vote?'

And it was then that she knew him. Or rather she

knew for certain that there was far more to this than Kedah was admitting to.

She did not blush. She had been trained not to react from an early age. And Kedah was the same— he never revealed fear. And so the hand on her arm did not tighten, nor did his breathing change, but as she carried on speaking she heard his heart rate quicken.

'And who would the people chose?' she asked.

'I believe...me.'

'No problem, then.'

'None.'

His response was measured and calm. Had they been having this conversation standing and facing each other, she would not have known of the nerve she had just hit, but his heart beat like a jackhammer in his chest.

'So why are you busy making billions just in case?'

He did not answer, and she lay there listening to the rapid thud of his heart.

'Does Mohammed have something on you?'

'I told you,' Kedah answered evenly. 'I don't regret my past.'

'I know there's a scandal looming.' Felicia smiled. 'I can smell them a mile off.'

There was.

For the first time in his life he needed advice. The question as to how to approach his mother had been rolling around in his head like a ball bearing in a pinball machine. Ideas were bounced around and were rapidly dismissed, but over and over he returned to one small corner that said he should speak with *someone*.

Who?

And, though he kept flicking the thought away, always the ball rolled back and settled in a pocket marked 'Felicia.'

He trusted no one, and yet…

'Felicia?'

She was sleepy and warm in his arms, though her low murmur in answer to her name told him she was awake.

'If I were to tell you something, would it remain between us?'

'Of course.' She smiled again. 'Hit me with it—a pregnant prostitute?'

'Excuse me?' he said, and then smiled in the darkness as he realised she was still trying to guess what his secret was. 'Was that before or after I got married in Vegas?'

She pulled herself from his arms and onto her elbow and she looked at him as his smile faded. The truth was scary sometimes, and she felt its brief threat.

'What is it?'

He shook his head, and Felicia knew when to remain silent. Any guessing now would only irritate, so she lay back down and played with his chest instead as she thought how best to respond.

'If you decide to tell me it shan't go any further.'

'Thank you.'

The gift of time was the best he had known, and he was grateful for it. He was aware it would be all to easy to say what was on his mind in this post-coital haze only to regret it later.

Even that didn't make full sense to him, though, for he did not usually indulge in pillow talk.

There was a small buzzing sound. It would seem that their flying time was nearly over. He reached out and flicked on a light and for the first time Felicia took in their splendid surroundings. Apart from the hum of the engines there was no sign that they were on an aeroplane.

The bed was vast, and rumpled from their love-making, and there was no place in the world she would rather be.

'Can we be late?' she asked, and lifted her face for a kiss.

Kedah was tempted to lift the phone beside the bed and inform the captain there was a change of plan, and yet some things needed to be faced.

'Get dressed,' he told her, though it was said with regret. 'I'll have your clothes brought through.'

'Can you at least wait until I'm in the shower?'

He smiled at her modesty, but did as she asked and waited until she had gone through to the bathroom before calling for her overnight bag to be brought to his bedroom.

Felicia washed her hair and dried it, and then she came out.

Kedah lay on the bed with his hands behind his head, clearly deep in thought.

Another buzzer sounded, and now it was Kedah who rose from the bed and headed to the shower as Felicia put on the robe she had chosen to wear. It was a dusky pink with long sleeves and a high neckline. From neck to floor the gown was done up with a row of embroidered buttons, each one individually made. Felicia had bought it while they'd been on their travels and was glad to be able to wear it. Again she chose to wear no make-up.

Kedah soon reappeared, wearing just a towel around his hips. He wished she did not move him so. For the first time in his life he perhaps regretted sex.

She had never looked more beautiful.

Her robe was a light crushed velvet, and it was subtle, yet he had touched each curve that it gracefully concealed, and his fingers itched to undo each button and return her to his bed. Her hair was loose and the air was fragrant with the perfume she had worn on the day they'd met.

Today was not one for distraction, and Felicia was proving a huge one.

He was reeling from coming so close to telling her the secret he had kept for all these years, and—more troublesome for Kedah—he was still dangerously close to revealing it now.

'Why don't you go and have some breakfast?' he suggested. 'I'll join you soon.'

Felicia nodded, unsure as to the dynamics between them, but just as she turned to go he caught her and pulled her back into his arms.

'You know that nothing can happen at the palace?'

'Of course.'

'We will leave straight after dinner. You will be taken to the offices to work there.'

'Kedah,' Felicia said, 'I don't expect us to leave the plane holding hands.'

'I know...'

She stepped from his embrace and went out to the lounge, where she was served breakfast. She was too consumed by Kedah to be embarrassed by the staff, but she was a little worried that they might gossip.

When Kedah came out of the bedroom she was about to voice her concerns to him.

Then she saw him.

The man who would be King.

Always he was beautiful—he was exquisite now.

The robe he wore was silver, and over that was an embroidered coat. His *keffiyeh* was black, and a heavy silver rope fell to one side. She had never seen him carry a sword and it unnerved her—for this was not a Kedah she had ever seen before.

Not just exquisite...he was truly out of her reach.

He was regal, imposing, and it was hard to imagine that less than an hour ago she had lain smiling in his arms.

An attendant served him strong coffee and he declined the sweet pastry she offered.

'They won't say anything?' Felicia checked, and he frowned. 'I mean, what happened won't get back to the palace?'

'Felicia, why do you think I use my own plane? You don't report to my father—none of my staff do. The only exception is Vadia.'

Kedah's success was not reliant on his title. But it was his hope for the future, and his heart belonged to the people he loved.

His words had come out perhaps more harshly than he'd intended—he had not meant to relegate her straight back to being staff—but he was having trouble with his worlds merging.

He had only ever brought Anu to his home, and there had never been anything between them. Anu was close to his mother's age and happily married.

Felicia would cause eyebrows to rise, and he wanted to spare her that shame.

Not that she knew that.

As they sat in silence Felicia looked out on Zazinia as the plane banked to the right and she got her first glimpse of his land from the sky. She understood a little more how thwarted Kedah must feel. It was stunningly beautiful, and yet so ancient that it looked almost biblical.

And then she saw the palace.

It was easily the highest point in the land, set on a cliff along a stretch of white beach.

And it was huge.

As the plane lined up for its approach Felicia re-alised the palace had its own runway, with several private jets that bore the royal coat of arms on their tails.

The landing was a smooth one, and soon they pre-pared to disembark.

'Am I to call you Your Highness here?'

'We have already addressed that—you can still call me Kedah.'

'And when we get to the palace am I to—?'

'Enough questions, Felicia,' Kedah snapped.

It was a stern reminder that they had left the bed-room, and Felicia felt the sting of her cheeks at his reprimand.

They stepped from the plane, with Felicia walk-ing a suitable distance behind him. Kedah was met by his personal aide, Vadia, whom Felicia had spo-ken to on several occasions.

There were no introductions for her, though.

The heat of the Zazinia air and the hot desert wind that whipped at her cheeks were not so hard for her to acclimatise to as her sudden relegation. An hour or so ago they had been in each other's arms, with Kedah almost revealing his darkest of secrets; now he didn't even glance over his shoulder as they stepped into the main entrance of the palace.

He indicated with a flick of his hand that she was to wait there.

A maid came over and she was informed in broken English that soon she would be taken to the offices in the royal wing.

And then Felicia stood, alone and ignored, as she heard a woman call out his name.

'Kedah!'

The woman who was walking towards him had to be his mother. She had the same winning smile as her son, and the robe she wore was a deep crimson. As Felicia glanced towards her she caught his mother's eyes and could see the question in her gaze.

Hurriedly she looked away.

Whatever was said was in Arabic as they embraced.

'Who is that?' Rina asked.

'That is my PA—Felicia.'

'Has Anu left?'

'No,' Kedah responded. 'But she wanted to pull back on the travel. Anu manages things in London now.'

'Well, your father and brother are looking forward to seeing you, Kedah. It has been far too long.'

Kedah doubted they *were* looking forward to seeing him, but they all tried to keep their troubles from his mother, and so he walked with her towards the main office.

Not once did he turn around.

Felicia felt less valuable than even his luggage, which was already being taken up to his suite. And it should not hurt quite so much, yet it did. To go from being his lover to less than nothing was not some-

thing she had prepared for. In all their time together
he had never made her feel worthless.

He did now.

The guards opened the doors as Kedah and Rina
approached, and inside Kedah kissed his father's
cheek and shook his brother's hand.

Kumu—Mohammed's wife—was there, and she
gave Kedah a small tap to the heart in greeting.

'Now we are all together,' Rina said, beaming,
'there is some good news that Mohammed and Kumu
have been waiting to share.'

She clapped her hands and Kedah stood silent as
his younger brother stepped forward.

'We have been gifted again,' Mohammed announced. 'In November we are expecting a child.'

'That is wonderful news.' Omar beamed, though
at the same time managed to freeze his eldest son
with a glare.

Congratulations were offered, and Kedah gave his
own. It would be another boy—of course it would.
Mohammed did everything to perfection, and had
already produced a potential heir and a spare.

All the right things were said, though, and Kedah
enquired after his young nephews.

'I hear you are looking to build another hotel in
Dubai?' his brother said.

'Another one?' Omar frowned.

'It is early days,' Kedah announced. 'I haven't yet
shown the plans to Hussain.'

That silenced his father for a moment.

Hussain and Omar had studied together, and on occasion Hussain had told Kedah about the fine plans his father had once had for his country.

Those days were long gone now.

A maid came in and announced that the portrait artist was ready, but Omar was not letting Kedah off that lightly.

'He can wait,' the King said. 'Now that he is finally here, I would like to speak with Kedah alone.'

'I don't mind staying,' Mohammed offered.

'That shan't be necessary,' Kedah said, and waited until he and his father were alone.

Omar cut straight to the chase.

'The elders are pushing for the royal lineage to move forward,' Omar said. 'Ours is a country that is divided, and there is unrest. Some want things to stay as they did under the rule of my father, and Mohammed is one of them—which is why the elders support him.'

'Your opinion is the one that matters,' Kedah pointed out.

'How can I support you when you are barely here?'

'You know why I stay away,' Kedah said. 'The people here need more infrastructure, healthcare, jobs—the list is endless. We have a country that could thrive, a tourism industry that could help people support their families. Instead they are poor while we continue to live in splendour. No, I cannot feast night after night in a palace when children go to bed hungry.'

'It is not so bad…' the King started, but then he saw Kedah's furious glare and hesitated.

It had been a long time since Kedah had lost his temper on this subject and Omar did not want a repeat.

'Kedah…' He trod more carefully. 'There have long been calls for the Accession Council to meet,' Omar told him. 'But it is becoming more pressing now.'

'Then give me the power I seek. Give me permission to make changes to our land and I shall return. You *know* that I would make a better Crown Prince and ultimately King than Mohammed.'

'How do I know that when you are never here? Prove your devotion…'

'I don't need to prove it—my country has my heart.'

'Choose your bride, come home and settle down. That would satisfy the elders for now, and perhaps delay the calls for the Accession Council to meet…'

'I don't need to appease anyone. I know my people—they want *me* as Crown Prince. If you vote otherwise at the meeting then I shall take it to the people to cast their vote, as is my right.'

'Have you *any* idea of the unrest that would cause?' His father was breathing rapidly. 'Kedah, why can't you just choose a bride and toe the line…?'

'What *happened* to you?' Kedah asked. 'Hussain

told me that when you studied together you had plans and dreams for our land… What happened to them?'

'The old King did not want change.'

'But *you* are King now. So why do you bow down to the elders?'

'They are wise.'

'Of course they are—but they are also staid. You are King. Your word is law and yet you choose not to use it.'

'It would be easier—'

'Easier?' Kedah interrupted. 'Since when did a king choose the easy option? Whatever hold the elders have on you, share it with me, and then together we can fight. But I shall not return to Zazinia just to sit idle and wait for you to pass.'

Kedah would not be pushed around by anyone. He knew his father was doing his best to protect his mother's reputation—he was quite sure that was why the King held back—but if only his father would voice the problem, together they could face the trouble.

Just so long as Kedah was indeed Omar's son.

There was a knock at the door and he knew there was only one person who would disturb an official meeting between the King and one of the Princes.

The door opened and the Queen stepped in, smiling widely.

'Rina,' the King scolded lightly, 'I am busy speaking with Kedah.'

'Well, the poor artist is waiting. He's so old that I am scared he will die if we keep him much longer.'

Omar laughed, and even Kedah smiled.

'Come, Kedah,' Rina said. 'I will walk with you.'

They walked through the palace and his mother stopped at a large floral arrangement and chose a bloom, which she placed in her hair, and then she selected a few more.

'It is so good to have both my sons home. Stay a while longer, Kedah.'

She was oblivious to the tension between him and Mohammed, and the terrible rumours had been kept from her. Kedah did not know how much longer they could remain so.

'I cannot stay. I have been away for a few weeks, and Felicia...'

He halted. Since when did he take into consideration the fact that his staff had not been home for a while?

And while Rina was oblivious to many things she was alert to others.

'Careful, Kedah.'

'Careful?' He frowned and stopped walking.

He almost wanted to confront her—to say that he was old enough now to understand an affair—but it was imperative, if he was to fight his brother, to know first that he was the King's son. But then he looked into her smiling chocolate-brown eyes that were flecked with gold like his and he couldn't do it.

There was a fragility to Rina—an air of impulsiveness and a little river of vulnerability that ran through her that sometimes darkened that winning smile.

If he confronted her now, Kedah would watch her fold and crumple. If he questioned her about what had happened all those years ago their relationship would never recover. That much he knew.

Yet if Mohammed called his lineage into question her shame would be held up for the elders and ultimately the people to discuss.

He was scared for his mother.

'Be careful with Felicia,' Rina said. 'Be careful with a young woman's heart.'

Kedah shook his head. His mother did not have to concern herself with his sex life, and especially not with Felicia's heart. This was a business arrangement, and if anyone could handle it, it was Felicia— she was the toughest person he knew.

'You don't have to worry about her.'

'But I do. You have never brought one of your lovers to the palace.'

They walked on and Kedah said nothing. But his mother was right. It was in part the reason he would not be staying longer. He wanted Felicia in his bed, and that could never happen here.

'You are choosing a bride soon,' his mother warned. 'It is not fair to her to be here.'

'Felicia is fine.'

Rina wasn't so sure. She had seen Felicia's angry

glare as Kedah had made her walk behind him and ignored her.

And now there Felicia was, standing on a balcony, looking out at the view.

'Think about staying for a little while, Kedah,' Rina said, and kissed his cheek. 'I miss you.'

'I know.'

'Come home.'

He wanted to.

'I cannot sit idle for years like…' He halted.

'Like your father has?'

He nodded, and after a moment of sad thought Rina cupped his cheek.

'I do understand.'

Could he ask his mother for the truth? If he *was* his father's son then he could confront the rumours and douse them before the sun went down on this day.

If he wasn't…?

Kedah was ready to know.

'Mother…' He stood there and felt as if he had removed his sword and now held it over her head.

'Yes?'

Rina smiled. And he did not know how to ask her.

'Why don't you give Felicia these?' she suggested.

'You tell me to be careful and then you suggest that I give her flowers?'

'I often pick some flowers to sit on Vadia's desk while she works.'

Indeed Rina did.

'I need to get on,' he said to his mother.

No, he would not go to Felicia with flowers.

Felicia didn't turn when he came to join her—she was still smarting. She was a very modern woman, and while careerwise she would have been fine walking two steps behind him and being ignored, having just left his bed she could not accept it—though she was doing her best not to let it show.

'I want you to take some photos of this wing while I go and have my portrait finished...'

'Sure.'

They walked around the Crown Prince's wing as the staff prepared his office and brought in the artist to add the final touches to the painting.

'I think this area could be better used,' he mused. 'Perhaps as a pool or spa area?'

Felicia tried to keep her features expressionless, though she was aghast at the very thought. It was an ancient palace and absolutely beautiful. To think he would consider tearing up these walls and floors to transform them into some modern gym was appalling.

'You don't approve?'

'I think that it's far too beautiful to risk spoiling.'

'You've seen my work?' Kedah checked, and she nodded. 'So why do you think I would ruin it? I want to enhance what is already here. I want somewhere I can live rather than a museum.'

They stopped by the portraits, and possibly she

could see what he meant. Cool grey eyes seemed to follow them, and they were a forbidding sight indeed.

'I'm meeting with Vadia in an hour,' Felicia said. 'We just spoke on the phone. She wants to take some time to go through your schedule. September is the King's birthday, yet that week you're booked to be in New York.'

'I have a friend's wedding.'

'Oh, and speaking of weddings… Vadia wants to go through potential dates for yours.'

She said it so calmly that Kedah honestly thought his mother was wrong and Felicia was fine with their arrangement.

'Tell Vadia that, given I haven't chosen my bride yet, it's a bit early to be discussing dates.'

'Sure.'

'I have a family dinner to attend after the portrait,' Kedah said. 'Your meal shall be served to you at your desk. Just call through with your order. We should fly out around midnight,' he told her. 'You'll be home by morning.'

But tomorrow was a day too late, Felicia thought.

If only this visit had been arranged for yesterday…if only she could have held out for a couple more days… Then she wouldn't be feeling as she did now.

She looked at the portraits of the men who had come before him. They were dressed in robes of black or white and the familiar chequered headwear.

Kedah wore a gorgeous silken robe and an embroidered coat.

Somehow, even traditionally dressed, he made a statement.

'You're going to stand out amongst the others,' she said.

'I always do,' he answered, and looked at the portraits of his father and grandfather. The fact that he dressed differently had little to do with it. 'I don't look like any of them.'

He walked off and Felicia stood there, frowning— not at what he had said, more at *the way* he had said it.

She knew she was already in too deep, yet as she looked up at the portraits he dragged her in ever deeper.

She was beginning to understand.

Kedah stood for his portrait.

The artist was indeed ancient, and it was hard to believe that those shaky hands could produce something so beautiful.

'I have painted your grandfather, your father, and now you,' the old man said as he added the final touches. 'I hope to paint the next Crown Prince.'

'It might be Crown Princess,' Kedah answered. He was bored from standing so long, and ready for a little disagreement, but the old man just smiled at the provocation.

'That is something to stay alive just to see.'

Yes, Kedah thought, the people really were ready for change.

The painting had been done over many sessions and Kedah, who hated to be still for more than a moment, had found the entire process excruciating.

'Just turn your face a little to the left,' the old man said. 'And look out to the desert.' The sky was orange and he wanted it to light the gold flecks in Kedah's eyes.

And so Kedah sighed and stared out to the desert. No wonder the portraits were of men looking stern, Kedah thought as he dwelt on his problems and pondered again discussing things with Felicia.

A woman's view on things might help, and she might know better how to broach the subject with his mother.

And, given her own family and her job, if there was anyone who would not be shocked by an illicit affair it was Felicia.

But could he trust her?

Yes.

It was a revelation, for since the day he had discovered his mother and Abdal his childhood innocence had faded and trust had rapidly left his heart.

He had thought it gone for good, but now he looked back on his time with her and their conversations. He remembered sitting in the restaurant as she'd revealed the dark part of her heart, and then smiled as he recalled her forthright observations about his hotels.

And then he remembered her lying in his arms, and how close he had come to confiding in her.

Then he thought of her beauty today.

The sun was setting and the desert fired red in the distance as the old man put down his brush and his work was finally done.

'Would you care to see it, Your Highness?' he offered, but Kedah shook his head.

'I shall wait until it is framed,' Kedah told him.

He did not want to stare upon the truth.

CHAPTER SEVEN

THEIR DEPARTING FLIGHT from Zazinia was very different from their outward flight. Despite the pilot's best efforts to climb above it, turbulence carried them home.

Kedah tapped his diamond, cursing the missed opportunity with his mother, and Felicia looked out of the window to the seemingly black lake of desert below. She was still angry about being ignored and dining at her desk alone, while cross with herself for expecting it could be any other way.

As they bumped through the sky she decided to try to do some work and put on her headphones. She would look at the presentation that she had been asked to send to Hussain. But, without thinking, she opened the file in the first email that Kedah had sent her.

Realising it was the one he had sent in error—the one he had told her to delete—she was about to exit from it when she paused.

She had sat through a lot of presentations these

past weeks. She had expected to see a proposal for the Dubai hotel and the walkway, and to label a few files, but instead she saw magic.

It was Zazinia, she quickly realised.

It was Kedah's vision of Zazinia.

With each passing frame the bare skyline was filled with graceful buildings, and each was a work of art in itself. Instead of gleaming silver or gold with mirrored windows, the buildings blended with the ancient surrounds. There were delicate artistic murals on the walls that faced the palace, and the city spread gently outwards rather than up. There were carefully thought out roads, railways and bridges to link communities, while the desert retained its remote beauty.

He had poured everything into this, Felicia knew.

It was a life's work in the making.

And she knew he had never meant her to see it.

She snapped off the presentation and then looked over. His eyes were waiting for hers to meet his. She pulled her earphones off, wondering if he somehow knew what she had just seen.

The truth proved to be just as disconcerting, and it troubled her how deeply he could bore into her heart.

'I apologise for the way I treated you back at the palace.'

Despite being strapped in, she almost fell off her chair in surprise. The apology jolted her, even if her expression barely faltered.

'I have never brought a woman there. Colleagues,

of course, but…' He gave a tense shake of his head. 'If there had been even a hint that we were involved then it could have made things awkward for you. I didn't handle it well.'

Please don't be nice, Felicia thought, because her feelings were so much easier to deal with when she was cross.

'Well, it's done now.' She shrugged. 'And I shan't be back there again.'

'I doubt there would be any reason…'

'No,' Felicia said. 'You misunderstand. I *shan't* be going back there again, Kedah. We all have our limits, and your treatment of me in Zazinia far exceeded mine. Anyway, there's no need for me to be there.'

'No.'

It had been too far out of her comfort zone. Had she only been working for him, she might not have liked it, but of course she would have accepted his treatment of her.

But they were lovers.

Oh, it was a business arrangement, perhaps, but still she could not flick a switch. She refused to go from being his lover to a servant who walked behind him, being ignored. His little hand-flick had incensed her.

An hour out of London the turbulence finally eased, and by then Felicia was dozing. Kedah went to his bedroom, but there wasn't time to shower so he just changed out of his traditional clothing into a suit.

He could have slept for an hour, maybe, but instead he sat on the bed with his head in his hands.

Despite his brave words, he did not know what his response would be should his father back Mohammed.

Should he risk his mother's past being exposed by taking it to a public vote? What if the title of Crown Prince wasn't rightly his?

Usually Kedah looked immaculate.

Not this morning.

London was beautiful, Felicia thought from the back of a luxurious car, and yet it wasn't the same as when she'd left. The last few weeks had been spent exclusively with Kedah, and nothing felt the same.

This wasn't a date. He didn't drop her home first. Kedah was both royal *and* her boss, so they pulled up outside his apartment and she got out and ensured all his luggage had been removed.

Here, they always said goodbye.

'I'm assuming that I've got the rest of the day off?'

'Of course.'

It had been a very long business trip, and new boundaries needed to be established now.

'I'll see you tomorrow at eight,' she said, and as she did so Big Ben chimed and they stood there. It was seven in the morning, which meant a separation of twenty-five hours.

'Come up,' Kedah said.

'I'm really tired.'

'I know you are.'

He could see the shadows under her eyes, and he was exhausted too. But the turbulence on the plane was nothing compared to now.

They were on the edge of being stupid.

Sleep-deprived, wanting, holding back...neither really knew.

She should run, Felicia thought. Jump in the car and go home.

Go to her mother's tonight for a timely reminder on what falling in love with a certain type of man could do.

But, truly, she didn't know how to play tough today—especially when Kedah spoke on.

'You said that if I decide to tell you it won't go any further. Does that still apply?'

And just when she knew she should walk away, he beckoned her in.

'You know it does.'

He took her hand as he signalled the driver to remove her cases from the car too.

She stood in the antique elevator beside him, and even then she knew she should get out.

But it wasn't curiosity that had led her back to him. It was desire.

Every minute available to them she wanted to claim.

She would heal later.

Felicia had been in his apartment a couple of

times, though never with Kedah there. Usually she went there to speak with a maid, or went with his driver to collect his luggage.

Now, she was a little unsure of her role as she stepped into the magnificent abode.

The drapes were open, revealing beautiful private gardens, and she gazed out at them as the driver deposited their bags in the hallway.

Felicia knew she wasn't here as his PA, and yet she wasn't quite sure if it was her troubleshooting skills that Kedah was seeking now.

'I'm going to shower,' he told her, and she nodded. 'Join me?'

She gave a tired laugh and carried on staring out of the window as Kedah headed off. His presumption should irk her, yet it didn't.

She wanted him, after all.

It was later that concerned her, not now.

Kedah walked into his large bathroom and removed his clothing. It should feel good to be home after all this time away, yet it never quite did.

Home was Zazinia.

He turned on the shower and the jets of water should have blasted him awake, but he was too tired for that. He stood soaping his body, still questioning the wisdom of telling the truth to another person.

But then he watched as Felicia, a little late, took up his offer to join him.

And for the first time it was good to be home.

'Wait,' he told her as she started to undress.

Kedah came out of the shower and she stood as he took care of the intricate buttons he had itched to undo so many hours ago.

This time he gave no orders. Instead he simply did what he must to get her naked. He peeled off her robe and then helped her out of her underwear.

'You're shaking?' he said, because he could feel the tremble in her as she stepped out of her knickers.

'I think I officially have jet lag,' she said.

She didn't.

Well, she probably did. But in that walk from the lounge through his bedroom to the bathroom she had known she was entrenching herself deeper into his life.

He lifted her hair and kissed her neck softly, deeply, intimately, in a way that made her dizzy. And she wished he did not take quite such care, so that later she could fault him, but instead he took her, tired and aching, into the shower.

First he washed her hair, and those strong fingers worked her into a quiet frenzy. He soaped her body and he missed nothing—not a finger, nor that patch of skin behind her knees that she had become aware of on the very first day they met.

And she did nothing. She didn't even touch him. She just felt the arousal that swirled around them thicken and knew of his increasing pleasure as his breathing tripped on occasion.

She faced away from him and he splayed her hands against the glass. He kissed down her back and it was the first time since childhood that Felicia had cried. Not that he could see that she did, for the water took care of that, and not that he could hear that she did, for she sobbed also with desire.

'Turn around.'

They were the only words spoken, and when she did she was met with a wall of muscle. He held her and lifted her hair and kissed her, so the sound of water was but a distant thrum. It was so distant that it took her a moment to realise that he had turned the taps off. Taking her hand, he led her dripping wet to his bed.

They would pay for this later, Felicia was sure. They would wake up in soaked sheets, with her hair in chaos, but she cared nothing about that now.

She shivered—not just from the cool of the air on her wet skin, nor her building need, but from the darkness of the bedroom that shut out the morning sun, from the upending of her senses.

In his room, she was deeper into his life.

He pulled back the covers and she climbed in, and then he wrapped her not in linen but in the cocoon of his body. He was barely on his elbows, their skin was in full contact, and his weight was pleasurably heavy upon her.

Then he took her, and Kedah had never meant to take her like this. He drove in on a kiss and told her her name. He told her just who he needed to chase away the demons.

And she said stupid words—like *yes* and his name.

All her anger and fury at being ignored and having to walk behind him was not eliminated by his kiss—in fact it was intensified. As he took her, hard and fast, there was almost a fight to the death taking place. Delicious anger burned and cleansed.

He pounded her senses until she could take it no more, and she came but did not surrender, even while moaning his name and unfurling at her core.

He met her, matched her, he filled her deeply and she lay there beneath him, breathless.

And she was still angry.

Did he think this was a part of the service? Did he think she could just give herself to *anyone* like that?

Clearly he did, Felicia thought, for she assumed all his lovers were treated to such intimate bliss.

She could never have known she was the first in this bed.

He rolled from her.

He had spent a lifetime wishing he had never opened that door, wishing he had never seen what he had. Now he checked that Felicia wanted to come further into his world.

'Do you want to know?'

She glanced at the clock by the bed and it told her it was nine.

Her cases were there in the hall. She could easily dress now, make some casual comment and tell him it would keep and head for home.

Get out now, while she still had a chance.

It was already far too late for that.

Her tears in the shower had left her surprisingly clear-headed, and she knew now she could not leave him by simple choice.

'Yes.' She turned and nodded. 'I want to know.'

CHAPTER EIGHT

'THAT ARTICLE YOU read on the day of our first meeting,' Kedah said. 'Do you have it?'

'It was taken down from the internet.'

'Come off it, Felicia.'

He knew that she was savvy and would have taken a screenshot, and of course she confirmed it. 'I've got it on my phone.'

'Take a look.'

He got out of bed and it troubled Felicia how little it bothered her that he went into her bag and took out her phone, which he handed to her.

'Have another read of it while I go and make coffee.'

She moved over to the side of the bed that wasn't damp from the shower and read again about the very decadent Sheikh Kedah.

'What do you see?' He brought in some drinks and then climbed in beside her on the dry side of the bed.

'There's nothing I don't know. They're hinting that the Accession Council should meet…'

'Read on,' Kedah told her, and she frowned and read down.

'There's just a picture of Mohammed and your father.'

'And what does the caption say?'

'"*Like father, like son.*"'

'There's a subtext there,' Kedah said. 'A warning that if I push for change then the truth might be revealed...'

Felicia frowned.

'The truth?'

'There is a rumour in Zazinia that I am not my father's son. It's not just that I look nothing like him— our visions are so different. Though the rumour persists, to date no one has dared voice it to my father or me. I believe soon they might. I need to be ready, and to quash it with the most withering riposte...'

She thought back to what he had said as they'd stood by those portraits—about looking nothing like any of them.

'I don't look like *my* father...' But Felicia knew there had to be more to it than just rumour, and so she asked the question no one dared. 'Is there a chance it might be true?'

'Yes,' Kedah told her, and he watched the swallowing in her throat. 'I caught my mother cheating when I was a young child.'

'Does anyone else know?'

Kedah thought back and shook his head. 'I was on my own when I caught them.'

'Does your mother know what you saw?'

Kedah didn't answer.

'Tell me what happened.'

'You don't need the details. I made a decision a long time ago never to speak of it.'

She saw his eyes shutter and Felicia let out a tense, 'What happened?' Then she continued. 'Tell me what you saw. You hate it when I discredit your work—well, don't dismiss mine. I deal with this type of thing a lot. Well, maybe not with royalty, but I know I can help. Though you have to tell me it all.'

She knew he didn't believe there was any difference she could make but, to his credit—or perhaps to hers—he told her some more.

'I was young.'

'How young?'

'Just turning three.'

He was hesitant to say more, but then he looked at Felicia. Yes, Matteo had been right about her. She was tough and experienced—he himself had seen that. And now they were lovers. But, more than that, he trusted her.

'The office where you worked yesterday…just outside the one where my portrait was done…?' He offered the location and Felicia nodded as her mind's eye went there. 'I was hiding from the royal nanny. My grandfather and father had been away and I didn't want to go and welcome them back, so I ran off and hid under the desk. I could hear noises coming from inside the office, and at first I thought my mother was hurt. When I opened the door she was being held by Abdal.'

'Abdal?' Felicia checked, but then, aware of her own impatience, she shook her head—she would find out in time. 'Go on.'

'Abdal walked off and she told me she had been crying and that he had been comforting her. She told me not to tell the King or anyone else. I don't think she knows that I remember.'

'What about the nanny?' Felicia asked. 'The one you were hiding from?'

'She came in then, and apologised for losing sight of me.' Kedah thought back. 'She was awkward, though I don't think she would have seen...'

'She might have seen Abdal leaving.' It was good that Felicia had been to the palace and could picture it properly. That corridor was a long one, and if the nanny had seen Abdal leaving then it might have been clear he had been alone with the Queen.

While the King was away.

It was immaterial now, but possibly this helped Felicia understand how important it was to Kedah that no one guessed what was between them.

They were still in bed together, and Felicia had never worked like this before.

They were trying to unravel the past, to work out how best to deal with the future.

Now she sat up cross-legged, with the sheet around her, trying to imagine that the Queen she had met would risk it all for a brief fling.

'Why, if you were only almost three when you caught them, do you think it was a prolonged affair?'

'You don't take the Queen over a study desk unless you're very sure...'

He looked up, and he saw that Felicia smiled.

It felt odd to smile about something so dark, and yet it helped that she did and so he told her some more.

'My mother comes from a much more modern country. Abdal was an aide also from there. He came to Zazinia to help with the transition and to ensure my grandfather upheld his agreements.'

'Did he?'

'Minimally. There was a lot of hope for change when the marriage took place, but little transpired. If he wasn't dead I would cheerfully kill him...'

Felicia didn't doubt him. Kedah's voice was ominous.

'Abdal had been in Zazinia ever since the royal wedding,' he went on.

'How soon after you caught them did he leave?'

Kedah thought back. 'A few days afterwards.' Even at such a young age he had served his mother a warning that day, and it had been heeded. 'I look nothing like my brother or my grandfather. He must have been a risk-taker to do what he did. So am I—'

'Kedah,' Felicia interrupted, in a voice that was terribly practical. 'Let's assume you inherited your risk-taking behaviour from your mother.'

He gave a reluctant smile, because he had never thought of it like that.

'What about a DNA test?' she asked. 'You'd know once and for all.'

He liked it that she was practical, that she didn't judge his mother or wring her hands, just got straight to the pertinent facts and seemed to sense how vital it was that Kedah knew where he stood.

'I've already had my profile done,' Kedah admitted. 'Anonymously, of course. But you've seen how it is there. Can you imagine me creeping around trying to find a comb?'

'You can get it from other things,' Felicia said. 'One of my other clients...'

His jaw gritted. He loathed thinking of her other clients and their scandalous pasts—and he loathed, more than that, that she had ever been close to them. 'I don't need to hear about them.'

'Maybe you do. With one of them I got a sample from chewing gum.'

'He's a *king*,' Kedah said.

'I get that. I'm just saying...'

'Why don't I pull on some gloves and offer him a stick of chewing gum or snip off some hair? Do you think no one will notice?' He lay back and tucked his hand behind his head as he tried to think.

If there was a solution to be had, he would have come up with it by now.

'I'm thinking of asking her.'

'Oh, no!' Felicia shook her head. 'Kedah, even if

she admits to the affair, she's never going to admit to *that*. Do you think your father knows about the rumours?'

'Possibly,' he said. 'But he still thinks my mother is perfection personified. He would defend her to the death. But I know that if he does then he could be made to look a fool. I need to know the truth.'

'Even if the result isn't the one you want?'

'I can handle the truth, Felicia.'

She believed him. 'But…?'

'I don't know that my mother could,' Kedah said. 'If even so much as the affair were exposed then my father would have no choice but to divorce her.'

'By the old rules?' Felicia said, and Kedah looked over to her. 'Does he love her?'

'Very much.' Kedah thought of how his father's face lit up whenever she came in the room. How he did all he could to shield her from the feud between her sons. 'I don't know how he'd be if the truth came out, though.'

He was done with talking about it.

'Come on,' he said. 'Sleep.'

And this time there was no thought of heading for her case, or making a feeble excuse that she needed to go home to water her plants.

Felicia slept.

CHAPTER NINE

FELICIA HAD NEVER known someone so able to separate the bedroom from work.

Kedah did it with ease.

And it helped.

At restaurants, her computer and her phone on the table served as a little wall between them. To remind her, as often as was necessary, that they were not lovers having lunch.

She was *working*.

Oh, but the nights!

In the evenings they ate at the best restaurants, without a computer between them, holding hands between courses and doing rude things under the table with their feet before returning home to his bed.

The bedroom was an entirely different thing. Her cases had long since been unpacked by his maids.

Her family and friends were very used to Felicia disappearing for weeks on end as she focused on her clients, so her absence was easily explained—even when she caught up with her mother for lunch.

'At least tell me who you're working for,' Susannah said.

'I can't just yet.' Felicia smiled and then looked at the time. 'I have to get back.'

Felicia *did* have to get back. Kedah had a two p.m. meeting with Hussain. But, knowing she needed supplies, after lunch Felicia decided to use lover's licence and dash back to her own flat.

Poor neglected flat, she thought as she grabbed some make-up wipes and tweezers from her bathroom cupboard. Two things that were sadly lacking at Kedah's.

Perhaps they should spend some time here...

And then she checked herself. It was easier that their time was spent at his apartment. She did not need constant reminders of him here when they were through.

And soon they would be.

Vadia's requests for a bridal selection date were almost daily now. The article that had been taken down from the internet was back up again, and there had been several more too.

Things were coming to a head, whether she wanted it or not.

Felicia opened up the cabinet and grabbed a fresh packet of contraceptive pills—the real reason she was there, for she was down to her last.

She went to grab some tampons too, but then remembered she'd already taken some to Kedah's last week.

She stilled as she realised she was down to her last pill and had nothing to show for it. Her tampons sat languishing in the glitzy mirrored cupboard in his bathroom.

Felicia stood for a very long moment and told herself it was the travel, it was exhaustion, it was being in love with a sexy sheikh who could never consider loving her back that had made her late.

And she *was* late.

Late with her period, late back from lunch.

And, because they kept things very separate, Kedah did not hold back from pointing this out.

'You're late.' He scowled.

'Indeed I am,' she responded.

'You haven't sent the file to Hussain...'

'No.' She sighed. She'd been too engrossed in that other file he'd mistakenly sent her to remember a small detail like that. 'I forgot.'

'Well, don't forget again,' he said, but then he halted.

He knew he was working her hard—both at work and in the bedroom.

Workwise... Well, he knew that time was running out, so he was trying to fit everything in.

And as for the other...

The same.

Still Felicia fascinated him. Still he wanted her over and over.

Usually his interest waned by the time the sun rose on a new day, but this fidelity trial was going exceptionally well.

* * *

Felicia did not wait for him to terminate the conversation. Every night she spent with him she felt as if she were handing over more and more of her heart, and she could not take it much longer.

She walked out and sat at her desk. She smiled at Anu, who brought some tea into her office and then left Felicia to work, but a few moments later Anu was back.

'Felicia...' She sounded concerned. 'That was Reception. Kedah's brother is here to see him, but he's in a meeting with Hussain and he told me that I am not to disturb him.'

'Well, he said nothing of the sort to *me*.' Felicia smiled sweetly as she reached for the phone, which made Anu laugh.

Kedah was not impressed. 'I said that I wasn't to be disturbed.'

'Well, you might change your mind for this. Apparently Mohammed is down in Reception.'

Kedah looked over to Hussain. His first instinct was to tell Felicia to let Mohammed know he was in a meeting and that he would see him when he was ready.

But there was no point.

This was no idle visit, and Kedah had to show he had no reason to delay or hide.

'He can come up.'

He spoke to Hussain. 'I am going to have to cut

our meeting short. It would seem Mohammed has flown in to speak with me. I hope you understand.'

'Of course.'

The men shook hands and suddenly, for Kedah, the design for a hotel in Dubai held little importance.

Hussain saw himself out of the office. He looked more serious than Felicia had ever seen him. Usually Hussain stopped and spoke, but today he just nodded to Anu, who also looked troubled.

Mohammed walked in, and when Anu did not move Felicia greeted the Prince and showed him through. 'Can I get you any refreshments?' she offered.

'No, thank you,' Kedah said. 'That shall be all.'

It was all supremely polite, but the air was so thick it was like closing the door on a tornado.

'Trouble is here,' Anu said once the door had closed.

'Not necessarily,' Felicia offered.

'I grew up knowing that this day would come.'

So had Kedah.

'This is a surprise.' Kedah's voice told his brother that it wasn't a particularly pleasant one.

'I only decided to come this morning,' Mohammed said as he took a seat. 'I sat in on a meeting about brides considered to be suitable as future Queen. It struck me as odd, given that I already have a wonderful bride, who would make an excellent queen, as well as two sons.'

'*I* am first in line,' Kedah answered smoothly. 'Why would you consider it odd?'

'Because I am the one sitting there discussing the future of our country and you are miles away, focusing on your own wealth.'

'As I have long said to our father, and to our grandfather before him, I am more than happy to devote my attention to Zazinia, and I shall do so when I am not thwarted at every turn. If I have to wait to be King to see my country flourish and thrive, then I shall do so—'

'I have been approached by Fatiq,' Mohammed broke in. Fatiq was a senior elder. 'I felt it only fair to warn you that there is a majority agreement amongst the elders that *I* would make a more suitable Crown Prince and King.'

'I could have told you that a decade ago.' Kedah shrugged. 'That is old news.'

'They feel that your interests are clearly removed from Zazinia...'

'Never.'

'And they suggest that it is time for you to step aside and make way for the most suitable heir.'

'Never,' Kedah said again.

'Some also say that I am the *rightful* heir.'

'Name them,' Kedah responded with a challenge.

Mohammed shook his head. 'I cannot do that. However, should an Accession Council meeting be called...'

'Why would that happen? Our father has stated

that once I choose my bride I will have his full support.'

'Kedah, we don't *want* it go to the Accession Council. You know as well as I do that there are things that should be left unsaid. You have the power to halt the elders.'

And Kedah saw his brother's game plan then. Mohammed wanted the threat of his mother's exposure to force Kedah aside.

He had chosen the wrong man, though, for Kedah would never be bullied.

'You really think I would step aside to appease the elders?'

'No, but I feel you would for the sake of our mother's integrity...'

Mohammed had intended to prompt his brother finally to back down. Instead Kedah picked up his phone and called the palace. He was through to the King in a matter of moments.

'I am calling a meeting of the Accession Council,' he said to his father, and he stared his brother in the eyes as he did so. 'This shall be dealt with once and for all. Do I have your support or do I not?'

'Kedah...' The King had known his youngest son had flown out and had been waiting for this call. 'There is no need to call for a meeting. I have told you—return to Zazinia and choose your bride, appease the elders...'

Kedah had heard enough.

'The meeting will be held at sunset on Friday.

You shall stand in support of your eldest son or not. If Mohammed is chosen it will not be left there. I shall take the decision to the people.'

He threw down the phone and looked to his brother. 'I mean it,' Kedah warned him.

'The elders say that if pushed they will demand a DNA test...'

He waited for Kedah to crumble, for the Crown Prince to pale, but his brother gave a black laugh.

'They embrace technology when it suits them.' He dismissed the threat with a flick of his wrist, though privately he fought to keep that hand steady. 'I am returning to Zazinia...'

'Even though you know what it might do to our mother?'

'Don't turn this onto me,' Kedah warned, and now he stood. 'Don't pretend for a minute that you are not behind this too. If and when I choose a bride—'

'You cannot!' Mohammed frowned, but backed off slightly as his brother approached. 'Why would you do that to her?'

'To whom?' Kedah frowned too.

'To your *wife*.' Mohammed had stopped even pretending he wasn't the one leading this coup. 'I was just saying yesterday to Kumu—*she* married a prince who might one day be King. Whereas *your* bride will marry the Crown Prince who might one day be a commoner. You are in no position to choose a wife.'

Kedah just gave another black laugh as he took

his brother by the throat. He, too, had stopped pretending.

'If my mother's name is ever discredited I shall have you thrown in prison.'

'You don't seem to understand, Kedah. The power won't be yours.'

And Kedah's response…?

It had been banter when he had said it to Felicia, but there was no hint of that now, and he watched Mohammed pale as he delivered his threat. 'Then I shall deal with you outside of the law.'

CHAPTER TEN

FELICIA SAT IN her office as Kedah's other world intervened.

Or rather his real world.

This was all temporary. They had always had a use-by date and she had to remind herself of that.

Not any more, though, for now there was no hiding from the truth.

From her office she could see Mohammed striding out, one hand massaging his neck, and she guessed there had been a tussle.

Felicia honestly could not deal with it now. She had been going through her calendar and trying to work out when her last period had been. Her world was a blur since she'd been working for Kedah.

She *couldn't* be pregnant?

Surely!

'Hey.'

Felicia looked up and there he was. 'How did it go?' she asked.

'He stated his case.'

And, after weeks of wanting to know more, and a career based on revelation, suddenly Felicia didn't want to know what had been said. She did not want to hear that their time was running out.

'Shall we go and get dinner?' Kedah suggested.

'It's not even five.'

'Let's go back to my apartment, then. We need to talk.'

'I have a meeting with Vadia soon.'

'Well, cancel it,' he said. 'We need to talk. Things are coming to a head back home. My brother has spoken with the elders. They want *him* as Crown Prince.'

She said nothing.

'My father seems to think if I choose a bride then we can put things off…'

Very deliberately, Felicia did not flinch.

'I have called for a meeting of the Accession Council this Friday at sunset.' For once the arrogant Kedah was pale. 'I shall leave on Thursday.'

'For how long?'

'I doubt it will be dealt with quickly. If the vote is in my favour I expect that things will get dirty, and the elders will do their best to question my lineage. I shall be busy there for the foreseeable future.'

'Where does that leave *me*?'

It was the neediest she had ever been, but thankfully Kedah took her at her selfish, career-focused best.

'Your contract is for a year. Whatever happens to me.'

It was like a slap on the cheek, but a necessary one, and it put her back in business mode.

'And if it goes in your favour?'

'Then it is time for me to step up.'

And, whatever way it went, Felicia knew things would never be the same.

'We need to sort out—' Kedah started, but she interrupted him.

'Not now.'

Felicia wanted to curl up on her sofa and hide from the building panic. She wanted a night spent with chocolate, convincing herself that she couldn't possibly be pregnant.

She had been right never to mix business with pleasure, because she was finding it impossible to think objectively now—and that was what he had hired her to do after all.

'I need to go home and think this through.'

'You can think it through with *me*.'

'No.'

She couldn't.

Because when she was with him feelings clouded the issue. A part of her didn't even *want* Kedah to be the rightful King, because if he was not that meant there might a chance for them.

Oh, surely not?

She had become Beth, Felicia realised, or one of the many others who had hoped against hope that things with Kedah might prove different for them.

She had fallen head over heels, even with due warning, and had hoped he might somehow change.

One day she would laugh, she decided.

One night in the future she would sit with friends, sipping a cocktail, and make them laugh as she told them how, even as he'd spoken of his future bride, even as he'd told her not to worry about her contract, she had hoped—stupidly hoped—there was a chance for them.

'I'm going home.' Felicia stood. 'I'll think about it tonight...' And then she did it. She offered the lovely wide smile that she gave to all her clients. The one that told them she'd handle this, that they could leave it with her. 'I'll come up with something.'

And Kedah said nothing. He just stepped aside as she brushed past.

He hadn't been asking her to come up with a solution! Conversation and something rather more basic would have sufficed. He'd never needed anyone in his life, yet tonight he needed Felicia Hamilton.

And she had walked off.

She'd had no choice but to.

It had been walk away or break down and cry— something she had sworn never to do in front of someone else, especially Kedah.

And so she headed for home, turned the key in the door, and stepped into the flat that had once felt familiar but no longer did.

She felt upended now.
At the age of twenty-six Felicia had fallen in love.
Real love.

CHAPTER ELEVEN

KEDAH ARRIVED FOR work a little later than usual the next day, and stepped out of the elevator to the aroma of coffee.

It had been a long night.

As much as it galled him to admit it, Mohammed had made a very good point—how could he marry when one day his title might be held up for question?

Kedah was proud, and the selection of royal brides from whom he would choose all expected him to one day be King.

His problems had kept him awake for most of the night, and this morning, just as he had been leaving, Omar had rung to try to persuade Kedah to call off the meeting. But he had refused.

It would just delay the inevitable.

He headed towards his office and there was Anu at her desk, drinking coffee. 'Good morning,' he said, and it took him a moment to register that Felicia wasn't there. Her office door was closed and the light was off.

'Good morning.' Anu went to stand up. 'Would you like coffee?'

'Later,' he said, and waved her to sit back down. 'You look tired.'

'I couldn't sleep,' Anu admitted. 'My mother called late last night and said there are reports that the Accession Council are meeting.'

'On Friday.' Kedah nodded and thought of Felicia's response—*Where does that leave me?* 'Anu, whatever happens your job is safe. I shall be keeping all my hotels and—'

'I'm not worried about my job, Kedah,' Anu said. 'Well, a bit… But my mother was upset and my father is too. I worry for my country. Growing up, we all looked forward to the day you would be King…'

'And I shall be,' Kedah said, though he could see that Anu wasn't convinced.

She would have grown up on the rumours too.

'I would like to fly back to Zazinia tomorrow, some time midmorning,' he told Anu. 'Can you arrange that, please?'

Tomorrow was Thursday. He could possibly have left it another day, but he wanted some time in his country to prepare for the meeting. Perhaps he would go to the desert and draw on its wisdom. He was very aware that tonight would be his last in London for the foreseeable future.

'Can you ask Felicia to come and speak with me as soon as she gets in?'

'Felicia's not coming in today,' Anu said. 'She just called in sick.'

Oh, no, she didn't!

Kedah walked into his office and, closing the door behind him, immediately picked up his phone.

The first time she didn't answer, but he refused to speak to a machine and so immediately called again.

Felicia stared at her phone and something told her that if she didn't pick up then Kedah would soon be at her door.

'Hi.' Felicia did her best to keep her voice crisp, but she had woken in tears and they simply would not stop.

'Are you crying?' Kedah asked.

'Of course not. I've got a cold. I've already explained that to Anu.'

'It's summer,' he pointed out.

'I've got a summer cold.'

'You were fine yesterday...'

'Well. I'm not today. Look, I'm sorry it's not convenient, but I really can't work. I need to take the day off.'

'Felicia...' Kedah's impatience was rising. She had swanned off before five last night and now, when he properly needed her, she had called in sick—with a cold, of all things. 'I want you here within the hour,' he told her. 'I have a lot to sort out. You know that. I fly to Zazinia tomorrow.'

'I can't come into work,' she responded. She didn't need to be looking in a mirror to know that her face was red and that her eyes were swollen from crying. 'I have to take today off. I believe my contract allows for sick days with a medical certificate?'

Felicia ended the call and turned off her phone. Refusing to lie there worrying, she hauled herself out of bed and dressed. Grabbing her purse, she headed out.

Oh, she was doing her best to reassure herself that it was travel and exhaustion that accounted for her being late, as well as the uncertainty of being head over heels in love with the most insensitive man in the world.

A man who could hold you in his arms while discussing brides.

A man who had told her to her face that an unplanned pregnancy wouldn't faze him and that the palace would 'handle' it.

Though for all he had stated it wouldn't be an issue, it might be a touch more scandal than he would want this close to a meeting of the Accession Council and the bridal selection.

Well, she didn't need Vadia to sort her out. Felicia would manage this herself!

She bought the necessary kit and, once home, did what the instructions said and waited, with mounting anxiety, trying to tell herself that she could *not* be pregnant.

Except just a moment later she found out that she was.

All the panic seemed to still inside her, and she

waited for it to regroup and slam back. She waited for the tears she had sobbed this morning to return with renewed vigour, but nothing happened. She sat there, staring at the indicator, trying to comprehend the fact that she was going to be a mum.

It wasn't something she'd ever really considered before. A baby had never factored in her plans.

Her career had always come first and relationships had come last.

Till Kedah.

Only she wasn't thinking about Kedah and scandals and the damage this might cause right now.

Instead she thought of herself and her own wants.

And she wanted her baby.

She wanted this little creation that had been made by them.

It was, for Felicia, a very instant love, for someone she knew she must protect.

And she had been told, though had never quite understood, that love was patient.

Could it be?

When she should be calling the doctor, or demanding Kedah's reaction, something told her that her baby would still be waiting on the other side.

There were other things that needed to be sorted now. It was time to focus on the job she had been hired to do.

Even though she had only known she was pregnant for an hour, right now Felicia needed to be a working mum.

Kedah's future might depend on it.

Yes, Felicia was *very* good at her job.

She went over and over their conversations and thought back to her time at the palace—it all came back to one thing.

Kedah needed to know, before he went into battle, whether or not he was the rightful Crown Prince.

Without that there could be no clear rebuttal, and if he *wasn't* his father's son...

Felicia sat in her little home study late into the afternoon. The shadows fell over her table and she was just about to put her desk lamp on when there was a knock at the door. She went down the hall, opened the door and signed for a box, which she took back to her study.

It was as if she had let in the sun, for now it streamed through the window, golden and warm. She smiled as she opened the box and took out a gorgeous basket. She looked at the contents.

There was a bottle of cognac and a glass, as well as a warmer. There was a dressing gown, silk handkerchiefs and organic honey. Felicia felt as though she was going to cry as she held lemons so perfect that they might have been chosen and hand-picked by angels.

There was everything you could possibly need if you did indeed have a cold and weren't in fact crying over Kedah.

What was it with him that he moved her so?

And not just her.

She thought of how he walked into a room and the aura Felicia felt she could see, how heads turned when he passed.

It wasn't just his beauty.

There was more.

When he gave his attention it was completely, whether it was to her or to a waiter. Kedah had a way of giving full focus, and she had never witnessed it in another.

Kedah was his father's son. Felicia was sure.

She was as certain as she could be that he had been born to be King.

But how could she prove it?

There was a note too, handwritten by him.

And this was much better than choosing from a brochure or a huge bunch of flowers.

She could imagine the courier waiting as he penned it, and knew that whatever happened she would keep it for ever—because while he made her cry in private, always he made her smile.

Felicia,
Of course you don't need a medical certificate.
I was just surprised that you were sick and dis-
appointed not to see you. Things are about to
get busy, but take the time you need to get well
and return when you are ready.
    It would mean a lot if I could see you tomor-

row before I leave for Zazinia. If not, I under-
stand, and shall be in touch soon.
Kedah.

Clearly he needed her on form to deal with the press and believed that she really had a cold.

Yes, he could be arrogant at times, she thought, but then he was so terribly kind.

And he must never know she had fallen in love with him.

It had never been part of the deal.

CHAPTER TWELVE

FELICIA WOKE LONG before her alarm, and after showering she dressed for battle.

And it *would* be a battle to keep her true feelings from him.

But there was work to be done and finally, after a long night spent tossing and turning, she had a plan.

She went to her wardrobe and chose the white dress she had worn on the first day they had met.

It was her favourite lie.

It made her look sweet when she wasn't.

It made her appear a touch fragile when in fact she was very strong.

And she was strong enough to get through this.

She rubbed a little red lipstick into her nose and saw the redness of her eyes had gone down, so hopefully it looked as if she were at the end of a cold rather than in the throes of a broken heart.

Instead of arriving at work early she lingered over her breakfast, and then headed to a very exclusive department store and waited until its doors opened.

There she made a purchase, before going to his office where the doorman greeted her as she walked in.

'Can I help with your bags?' he offered.

'I'm fine, thank you,' she responded.

She would not let the bag and its contents out of her sight for even a moment.

It was far harder than facing the press—far harder than anything she had ever done—to walk out of the elevators with a smile and greet Anu, who looked as tearful and as anxious as Felicia felt on the inside.

'Is he in?' Felicia asked.

'He flies in a couple of hours.' Anu nodded. 'I just took a call from a reporter. He was asking for confirmation that he is flying today to Zazinia. I don't want to trouble Kedah with it, but I don't know what to say...'

'Just tell him that for security reasons you are not at liberty to discuss his movements,' Felicia answered, and then she looked at Anu's crestfallen face. 'Have some faith—Kedah will be fine.'

'You don't know that.'

'Of course I do.'

'You didn't grow up in Zazinia,' Anu said. 'The people there have always feared this. You don't know what is about to come...'

So Anu knew of the rumours, Felicia realised. Possibly the whole country did, and had been waiting for the black day when their Golden Prince was removed.

'When does he leave?'

'At midday.'

As Felicia headed towards Kedah's office Anu, the gatekeeper, stopped her. 'He said that he doesn't want to be disturbed.'

Felicia nodded, but would not be halted. 'I need to speak with him.'

She knocked on the door and when there was no response opened it. Kedah was on the phone, and he gestured for her to take a seat and then carried on speaking in Arabic for the best part of ten minutes before ending the call.

'Are you feeling better?' he checked.

'Much.' She nodded.

'Good—because the press have got hold of it already and my staff are starting to become concerned. Let them know that nothing has changed and—regarding the press—clarify, please, that it was I who called for a meeting of the Accession Council...' He stopped talking then and came around the desk. 'I didn't think you were coming in.' He went to take her in his arms. 'It's good to see you.'

Felicia pulled back. She could not take affection and also do what was required.

'Kedah, I've been thinking. Take me with you to Zazinia.'

'Felicia, I am going to be busy, and you know as well as I do that when I am there we can't do anything. Anyway, you said you'd never go back.'

'I know I did, but I'm not asking you to take me there for a romantic holiday. Kedah, if you knew for certain that you were your father's son, would it change things?'

'Of course.' He nodded. 'I am fighting blind at the moment, but…' he shook his head '…there is no way to find out unless I speak with my mother.'

'And we both know that no good can come from that.'

He didn't look convinced.

'Kedah, I've worked with people who've been caught red-handed and they'll all admit to once, but…' She shook her head. 'You need irrefutable proof—DNA testing.'

'I've told you—I couldn't get a sample without his knowing.' Kedah pressed his fingers to the bridge of his nose. 'Soon the elders will call for one.'

'Then find out *now*.'

'Ask him?'

'No.' Felicia shook her head. 'I doubt your father would want to know, unless forced. What if you asked him to come to your office?'

Felicia took a large box from the bag she had carried in and opened it. Along with a stunning crystal decanter and glasses there was a pair of white cotton gloves.

'I've got the buffering solution. I can prep the glass, and if he takes a drink from it I can fly straight back and have the test done. You said they already have your profile?'

Kedah nodded to that question, but then he shook his head. It could never work 'Felicia, you've seen how it is there. There is no way he would come into my office for a discussion, let alone stay long enough to have a drink. No, he would ask me to meet with him in his.'

'What if you had your office set up for a presentation?'

Kedah looked at her. 'What sort of presentation?'

'The one you've spent years working on—your hopes for Zazinia. Your vision for your country. All the plans you have made.'

All the plans that had been knocked back. 'I told you to delete that file.'

'Since when did I do as I was told?' Felicia shrugged. 'And I'm glad I watched it...'

'You watched it?'

'Of course I did.'

Of course she had, Kedah thought. This was the woman who had taken a screenshot of that article that had only briefly appeared online. He was a work project, a problem to solve, and for a while he had forgotten that.

'Aside from obtaining a DNA sample, I think it's something that your father ought to see. He needs to know what he's taking on—or turning his back on.'

Kedah had grown too used to the other side of Felicia—the softer side he sometimes glimpsed—not the very tough businesswoman she was.

And this, although private, *was* business.

The business of being royal.

'Show it to him,' Felicia said. 'We can set up for

a presentation in your office and ask him to come and view it. It goes on for an hour…'

It could work, Kedah realised. By the time the Accession Council met he could know the truth.

'Whatever the result, I shall fight for my people.'

'Ah, but it will make it so much easier, Kedah, if you're able to laugh in Mohammed's face…'

'Assuming the result is the one I want.'

'And if it's not?'

'I can handle the truth, Felicia.'

Could he?

She thought of the baby within her and wondered for a brief moment if it might be better to tell him— but then, in the same instant, she changed her mind.

Kedah needed to find out who his father was before she told him that he would soon become one.

There was no question of them whiling away the flight in the bedroom.

Kedah had not only his presentation to his father to edit, but also his speech for the Accession Council to prepare.

Aside from that, Felicia didn't know if she could risk being close to him right now without confessing her own truths.

Not just the baby, but the fact that she loved him.

So she put herself firmly into Felicia mode.

Or rather the Felicia he had first met.

She only had one robe that complied with the

dress code in Zazinia, so an hour from landing she went and changed into the dusky pink one.

Her hands were shaking as she did up the row of buttons and her breath was tight in her lungs. She feared that he might come in, for she was not sure she possessed the strength not to fold to his touch.

He did not come in.

Oh, he thought about it, but he didn't dare seek oblivion now. He knew he had to keep his mind on the game.

God, but he wanted her.

'Still working that worry bead?' she teased when she came out from getting changed and saw him tapping away.

'I told you—I never worry.'

'Liar.'

'I don't worry, Felicia. I come up with solutions. I've known for a long time that one day this would happen. While the outcome might not be favourable, I've prepared for every eventuality. I'm a self-made billionaire. I'll always get by.'

He flicked the diamond across the table to her and Felicia picked it up.

'It's exquisite.'

'When my designs for Zazinia were first knocked back I spoke with Hussain. He had studied architecture with my father, and when I told him the trouble I was having he said his struggles for change had been thwarted too, and he would not let history be repeated. He invited me to come in on a design with him in Dubai. It was my first hotel, and a stunning success. Back then I sold it. I had never had my own money. I cannot explain that… I was royal and rich, but to receive my first commission brought a freedom I had never imagined, and with the money I bought this. I know each time I look at it that, if need be, I can more than make my own way.'

'People will be hurt, Kedah, even if the result is what you want. If Mohammed discredits your mother…' Felicia had thought about that too. 'She will be okay. It would be awful for a while, but—'

'No,' Kedah interrupted. 'She would *not* be okay. She isn't strong in the way your mother is.'

Felicia looked up from the diamond she was examining. She had never heard her mother described as strong; in fact she had heard people suggest she was weak and a fool for standing by her father all those years.

'It must have taken strength of character to go through all she did,' Kedah said, and after a moment's thought Felicia nodded. 'My mother doesn't have that strength.'

It wasn't something that had ever been said outright, yet he had grown up knowing it to be true.

'I remember when my father went on that trip. His last words were, "Look after your mother."' Kedah hadn't even been three. 'My father always said it, and I always took it seriously. She is a wonderful woman, but she is emotionally fragile. All the arguments, all the politics—we do our best to keep them from her.

She does so many good things for our country. She worries for the homeless and cries for them, pleads with my father to make better provision for them. She takes their hurts so personally...'

There was no easy answer.

'She'll be okay,' Felicia said again, and watched as Kedah gave a tense shrug.

Had she even listened to what he had just said? he wondered.

She had.

'Your mother *shall* be okay, Kedah, whatever happens. It sounds to me as if she has the King's love.'

Kedah nodded. 'She does.'

Rina, Felicia thought, was a lucky woman indeed.

Kedah went back and forth to his country often. Usually they were short visits, so that he didn't get embroiled in a row, but he was a regular visitor and so as he stepped out of the plane he knew what to expect.

Or he thought he did.

But this time, as Kedah stepped from the plane it was to the sound of cheering. From beyond the palace walls the people of Zazinia had gathered to cheer their Prince home.

They wanted Kedah to rule one day, and it was their way of letting the Accession Council know that he was the people's choice.

Kedah would make the better King.

'Kedah!' Rina embraced him, but she had a question to ask. 'Why now?'

'Because the elders have long wanted Mohammed and it is time to put this to rest once and for all.' He stepped back. 'I have some work to do. I shall be in my wing.'

'Kedah…' Omar came out to greet his son.

'I would like to speak with you,' Kedah told him.

'Of course,' the King agreed. 'I have much to discuss with you also. Come through to my office.'

'I would prefer that we speak in mine,' Kedah responded but Omar shook his head.

'We shall meet in mine.'

'I have something I want you to see.' Kedah refused to be dissuaded. 'I will go and prepare for you now.'

He didn't even turn his head to address Felicia.

He just summoned her in a brusque tone and gave that annoying flick of his wrist.

He offered a small bow to his parents and walked off, with Felicia a suitable distance behind him.

Up the palace steps they went, past the statue where as a child Kedah had hidden, and then past the guards and down a long corridor. Felicia understood now why he wanted these offices destroyed, for events there had caused so much pain, and possibly were about to cause more—not just for Kedah, but for his family and the people.

He closed the heavy door behind them and dealt with the projector and computer as Felicia pulled on gloves and pulled out a decanter and glasses and filled them.

'If he asks for another drink don't top it up—let him do it. You don't want anything from *you* on this glass.'

'He'll call for a maid to do it,' Kedah said. 'He is King.'

Felicia was confident that Omar would not be calling for a maid. After all, she had seen the presentation and had no doubt Omar would sit transfixed as he watched it, just as she had.

'Are you nervous?' she asked, and then went to correct herself. Of course he wasn't nervous—Kedah never was. Yet he surprised her.

'Yes.'

It was possibly the most honest he had ever been. In some ways more open than he had ever been, even in bed. She went straight over to him and as easily as that he accepted her in his arms.

Kedah took a long, steadying breath as she leant on his chest. Here, once the scene of such devastation, he found a moment of peace.

'I'm sure the result will be as you wish it to be.'

'No one has seen my work before...'

'Kedah?' She looked up to him. 'It might not count for much, but *I've* seen it and, for what it's worth, I thought it was amazing.'

He was about to say that he hadn't meant it like that—more that no one important had seen it—but then, as he stood there, holding her, it dawned on him that the presentation had been watched by someone *very* important to him.

'Did you watch it all the way through?'

'Yes.'

'And…?'

'The truth?' Felicia checked, and he nodded.

'I saw it first by mistake and I have watched it many times since. The designs are stunning, Kedah.'

'I thought you said my work was impersonal?' he teased, and Felicia looked up.

'Your vision for Zazinia isn't work.'

It was everything.

There was the sound of the guards standing to attention and, when he would have preferred to hold her for a moment longer, Kedah had no choice but to let her go.

Felicia's eyes were glassy and, rather than let him see, she busied herself, walking over to check the projector was set up correctly and that everything was in place.

And then the door opened and in came Omar the King.

'Thank you for coming,' Kedah said, and he stood proudly. He had possibly been preparing for this moment for most of his adult life. Not just the confrontation, but sharing his vision for Zazinia with his father. 'I have something I would like you to see.'

'Not without first hearing your choice.' Omar thrust a bundle of files onto Kedah's desk. 'This is a shortlist of suitable brides.'

Even though Omar spoke in Arabic, this was not something Kedah wanted to discuss with a certain person present. 'Felicia, could you excuse us, please?'

'Of course.'

Omar hadn't even noticed that a lowly assistant was present, but he simply stood until she had left and the door closed quietly behind her.

Kedah broke the silence.

'If I choose a bride, then I shall have your full support at the Accession Council tomorrow?' he checked, and then let out a mirthless laugh at his father's lack of response.

He knew for certain that his father was bluffing, for he saw a rare nervous swallow from him as he reached for the files as if to peruse them.

'I need to know that, once I'm married, I shall have your approval to make the necessary changes...'

'First things first,' Omar said.

'Isn't that what *your* father said to *you*?' Kedah asked. 'Choose a bride, produce an heir, and *then* we can talk?'

Omar did not respond.

'Yet nothing got done, and all these years later still there is little progress in Zazinia...'

'I ensured an improved education system,' Omar interjected. 'I pushed for that.' Yet both men knew that he had pushed for little more. 'The King did not want change,' Omar said.

'What about *this* King?' Kedah asked, but again there was no response. 'Please,' Kedah said, 'have a seat.'

He dimmed the lights in the office and took a seat himself as the presentation commenced.

Kedah looked over to his father, but the King gave no comment—though he did, Kedah noted, take a sip of his drink. And, while that was supposed to be the reason they were there, suddenly his father's reaction to the presentation was more important to Kedah.

Felicia had been right. His father needed to see this.

And there it all played out.

Like golden snakes, roads wove across the screen and bridges did what they were designed to—bridged. Access was given to the remote west, where the poorest people fought to survive, and somehow it all connected.

Schools and hospitals appeared, and within the animation teachers, doctors and nurses walked. There were animated children too, playing in parks. Now, hotels rose, and there were pools. Restaurants and cafés appeared on bustling evening streets.

And the King sat in silence.

Kedah watched as his father took a drink, and another, yet made no comment. An hour later, when an animated sun had set on a very different Zazinia from the one they knew and the presentation had ended, it was Omar who stood and opened up the drapes.

Still he offered no comment. Omar just stared out to the golden desert beyond and it was Kedah who spoke.

'That is what you deny your people. All this is achievable and yet you do nothing…'

'No—'

'*Yes,*' Kedah refuted. 'Turn around and tell me that Mohammed would make the better Crown Prince.'

Omar did not.

'Turn around and tell me that you don't want a glittering future for our people.'

'That is enough, Kedah,' Omar said, but Kedah had not finished yet.

He picked up the files and held them out for his father. 'As I said to you when I was eighteen, you shall not force me to take a bride. I will never be pushed into something that is not of my choice. If you want me gone then say so, but let us stop pretending that it has anything to do with my choosing a wife.'

Kedah tossed the files down on the desk in frustration as again his father said nothing. He simply walked out.

He had shown his father his best—the very best of his vision, all that he hoped to achieve—and his father had offered no comment.

Felicia was startled when the office door opened unexpectedly. She did not receive any greeting from the very angry King who stalked past.

She had been seated at the very desk where years ago Kedah had once hidden, and now she took the same steps that he had at three years old—though she opened the door with greater ease.

'How was it?'

Kedah shrugged. 'Hopeless.'

'He didn't have a drink?' Felicia checked, and then Kedah remembered the real reason for the meeting.

He looked over to his father's glass, which was empty.

'I meant that the presentation was hopeless. He's never going to change his mind.'

Felicia pulled on her gloves and popped the glass into a clear bag, and then another, then placed it in her purse. On the desk she saw that there were some photos of dark-haired and dark-eyed beauties. One of them, no doubt, would be his bride.

Kedah was too incensed by his father's lack of response to notice where her gaze fell. His mind was on other things. 'What am I fighting for?' Kedah asked, and for the briefest moment he wavered where he had always been resolute. 'Am I the only one who wants change?'

'Your people want it also,' Felicia said. 'I heard them cheering you, Kedah.'

She was right—it wasn't just his ego that insisted he could do things better than his brother. And after his father's pale reaction to the presentation it was as if she blew the wind back into his sails.

'I am going to speak again with Mohammed,' Kedah said.

'Do so,' Felicia agreed. 'I'm going to head back to London.'

She was meeting a courier at Heathrow, who would take the glass to a laboratory where the samples would be analysed.

'I'll call you as soon as I get the results.'

And this was it, she realised. It was the very last time she would be in Zazinia—for certainly she would not travel here as his PA once Kedah had chosen his bride.

'Don't leave now.'

Kedah stood and came around the desk. He felt her resistance when he took her in his arms.

His fingers went to her chin and he lifted her face to meet his gaze. He was going to kiss her, she realised. Right now, when she was doing all she could not to break down.

'I have to go.'

'Not yet.'

His mouth was fierce and claiming, and she tasted salt at the back of her throat as she squeezed her eyes closed and held on to the tears he must never see her shed.

'Not here,' she said.

'Yes, here.'

He did not want her gone.

He could not picture the future. He just wanted a moment of the oblivion that they created together. So he did what Abdal should have done all those years ago.

Felicia stood as he walked over and turned the lock on the door.

Kedah turned her on in a way no one else ever had or ever would. He tossed his sword to the floor and was opening his robe as he walked back towards her.

His passion was so fierce and overpowering. His hands were at the buttons of her robe and he was holding back from tearing it open.

And she loathed herself for wanting him so badly.

Even with his future wife's photo on the desk she would do this. She *would*, Felicia decided as he lifted her onto the desk. Now, while she didn't know his wife's name, she would be taken for the last time.

His hands ruched up the skirt of her robe and lifted it over her thighs, and perhaps Kedah was aware that this was the last time because impatient fingers were tearing at the buttons.

She had to walk out of this office soon, so she tried to assist him. But the buttons gave way so that her legs and chest were exposed and he pulled down the cups of her bra. There was no time to take off her knickers. His erection moved the slip of fabric aside and he stabbed into her.

Felicia sobbed as he filled her.

Their mouths were frantic and bruising in their fast, urgent coupling.

He thrust hard, then pressed her so the desk was hard against her back and her hair splayed out. Now he tore at her knickers, and the sight of them, of himself deep inside her, almost made him come. It was intense, it was fast, and as he scooped her up her legs

wrapped around him and she bit his shoulder to fight
the scream as her body beat with his.

And it could never be over—and yet it was.

He was lowering her down, and she rested her
burning face against his chest and listened for the
last time to his heart. She told herself that she would
never succumb to this bliss again.

'Felicia...'

She peeled herself from him and started to do up
her robe. She wanted to be away from Zazinia, in the
safety of the plane and then back in London. There
she could sort out her head.

'I'd better get going.'

'In a moment. But first...'

'Kedah, the plane is waiting—there's a courier at
the other end. If there's to be any hope of getting the
results back in time...'

'Can't you stop thinking about work?'

'You *are* work, Kedah.'

Felicia took a mirror from her bag and ran a comb
through her hair, and she saw her own lips start to
tremble as he spoke on.

'In that case, if all goes well, then I am going to be
spending a lot more time here in Zazinia. I will need
someone to help with my overseas investments, and
there will be an opening for an executive assistant...'

And briefly she allowed herself to glimpse it—
an amazing career, a stunning flat and a night with
Kedah whenever time allowed. A part-time father...
yet she would be his full-time mistress...

She snapped the compact mirror closed and managed to sneer as she faced him 'You mean an executive *whore*?'

'Felicia...'

'I have to go.'

She really did—because otherwise she would say yes to him. If she stayed for just a few moments longer she would accept his crumbs.

'I'm going to go.'

'Of course.' He nodded.

'I hope you get the result that you're hoping for.'

And they were through.

She had but one more smile left in her, and she gave it to him now as she held up her bag.

'My work here is done,' she said.

'No,' Kedah said. 'You will be back in the office tomorrow. I employed you to look out for my people. This was...' He hesitated. 'A personal favour. Thank you.'

He could not quite believe that she knew. That he had asked for and received her help.

'I trust you, Felicia.'

And she waited for him to warn her, to remind her that if she let him down then she would be dealt with 'outside the law', but there was no postscript.

'I hope it all goes well,' she said.

And maybe he shouldn't trust her, because right then she had lied—for there was a part of her that *didn't* want him to be Crown Prince.

No.

She wanted what was best for him.

'Hey, Kedah?' Felicia said. 'For what it's worth...' This was the hardest thing she had ever said, the least selfish words she had ever spoken, because she was very good at her job, and she could see another route even if the news for Kedah was not good. 'It's very hard to dissuade a loyal public.'

Kedah frowned.

'Your people know the rumours and yet they still cheered you home. Whatever the result, you can still fight.'

She walked out and she saw that Mohammed was deep in conversation with Kumu at the end of the long corridor. When he saw Felicia approaching Mohammed stalked off, leaving Kumu by the large statue at the top of the stairs.

'Are you leaving?' Kumu asked, for she had heard that Kedah's jet had been prepared to fly out and Mohammed had asked her to glean more information.

'Yes...' Felicia smiled politely, about to carry on down the stairs. But even if Kedah wouldn't let her help, it didn't mean she couldn't try. And so she paused and turned around. 'It's a relief, actually,' she said in a low voice, as if confiding a secret.

'A relief?' Kumu frowned, a little taken aback but curious.

'I always worry that I'll say the wrong thing,' Felicia admitted.

'The wrong thing?'

'You're very used to royalty...' Felicia sighed. 'It's

just all so new to me. I keep worrying that I'm going to mess things up. I mean, King Omar has been perfectly kind, and he seems lovely—you just have to see how devoted he is to his wife to know that. Even so, I would *hate* to be the one to offend him.' She gave Kumu an eye roll. 'I mean, after all, he *is* the King.'

Kedah walked out of his office just in time to see the very end of a conversation between Kumu and Felicia, and almost instantly he doubted his thought process. Now Felicia was smiling and walking down the stairs, as confident as ever. Kumu, on the other hand, stood looking worried and clearly more than a little perplexed.

She hurried off, but Kedah's attention was no longer on Kumu. Instead he was looking again at Felicia.

Her slender frame packed a punch even from this distance. Confident, collected, she walked towards the grand entrance and nodded for the guards to open the doors. In her bag was the glass, the answer, but that wasn't all that was on Kedah's mind.

Yes, he would have to select a bride—and, given her response, that meant this was the end.

They were over—just as he had told her from the start that they would be.

'Felicia...'

The Queen called out to her as Felicia walked to the car.

'Your Majesty?'

'You're leaving already?'

'Yes, Kedah needs me to go back to London.'

The Queen frowned, for she had rather thought Kedah might need someone on his side here, for when the Accession Council met.

Felicia was driven the short distance to the private jet, which she boarded. It felt so odd to be there without him. Over the last few months they had flown together on many occasions.

The plane felt lonely without him.

Her *life* would from this point on.

'There's a slight delay getting clearance,' the steward informed her. 'It shouldn't be too long.'

But Felicia could no longer hold it in.

'I'll be in the bedroom. Call me when we're ready to take off.'

Felicia headed to the bedroom suite and lay on the bed and allowed the tears to come.

Oh, and they did come.

Except the slight delay wasn't in order to get clearance from Air Traffic Control—it was caused by a certain Crown Prince who did not like it that she had gone.

He was thinking of her on the long flight to London when, in truth, he would far rather she was here. For a moment he even considered the possibility of someone else taking the glass to have it tested.

But, no, that couldn't work. It would mean involving another person, and Kedah wanted it kept just between them.

She was crying too hard to hear her phone, but then there was a knock at the door.

'Kedah wishes to speak with you,' the steward informed her, and gestured to a phone by the bed.

Felicia furiously wiped away her tears and blew her nose before picking up.

'Hello?'

'Hey,' Kedah said.

'What do you want?'

Kedah had been about to talk dirty, to tell her to get back this minute, or maybe to be honest and tell her he wasn't ready to let her go. Then he heard her slightly thick voice and knew that unless Felicia had the most rapid-onset cold in medical history she was crying.

Which meant she'd been crying that other time. He knew that now.

It would seem that she did have a heart after all.

'How long will the results take?' he asked, and Felicia frowned.

Why would he ask when they'd already been through this numerous times?

'Overnight,' she answered. 'The results will be couriered to your office, hopefully by lunchtime in the UK.' Which would be late afternoon in Zazinia— just a few hours before the Accession Council met.

A few hours before he was expected to choose his bride.

'Felicia?'

'I think we're about to take off,' she lied. 'Speak soon, Kedah.'

CHAPTER THIRTEEN

KEDAH WAS VERY used to women falling for him.

He *wasn't* used to them proudly walking away.

He looked at the slight chaos their lovemaking had created and righted the crystal decanter that had toppled over. Then his eyes took in the files and the photos of the women his father wanted him to choose from.

Felicia had seen them, he was certain.

Their lovemaking had been fierce and angry, and now possibly he understood a little more why.

Yet she had known all along that he was to marry and had seemed fine with it.

Possibly she wasn't so assured after all.

Even though he generally didn't use it, Kedah was tempted to summon the royal jet, so he could be in London, or nearly there, when she landed. He needed to speak with her—he wanted to know what her tears meant exactly.

He needed space, and so he walked along the pristine white beach. Suddenly everything had changed.

Always he had wanted to be King; he had spent his life knowing it could be taken away and protecting himself from that possibility. Now, when the coming days should have his full attention, when he should be devoting every thought to the potential battle ahead, he was staring up at the sky that carried her.

He *had* chosen wisely.

Kedah had protected all the people he loved and cared for in this. Tomorrow, when the press were crawling and the staff were afraid, he would ensure that the best of the best knew his business inside out.

He knew Felicia could face this crisis.

In these past months she had crept into his heart, and now she belonged there so absolutely that it had taken her leaving to expose the fact.

And her tears made him believe that she loved him too.

What to do?

Omar stood in his own office, looking out on Zazinia and thinking of the presentation his eldest son had just shown him. He saw Kedah walking along the beach alone. As always, he cut an impressive figure, but for once his son's stride was not purposeful, and instead of looking out to the land he so loved Omar saw Kedah pause and gaze out to the ocean and the sky.

The King did not turn his head when the door opened and Rina stepped into his office. Instead he focused on his eldest son. There was a pensive air to him, and the set of his shoulders showed he carried a weight that was a heavy one.

Kedah was the rightful Crown Prince. Omar knew that.

Yes, the road ahead might be easier if he followed the elders' wishes and stood behind his younger son, but it would be the wrong decision.

He turned his head a little as Rina came in and walked over to stand by his side. She stood quietly beside him, watching their son, who cut a proud and lonely figure as he walked.

'Felicia just left,' Rina said.

'Felicia?' Omar frowned, for he had no idea who his wife was referring to.

'Kedah says she is his PA, but I am certain there is more to it.'

'Nothing can come of it. There are many brides that would be far more suitable.'

Omar's response was instant, but then he felt his wife's hand on his shoulder.

'I am sure plenty say the same about me,' Rina said. 'There are many who don't consider *me* suitable.'

So rarely did they touch on that long-ago painful time.

'You are a wonderful queen.'

'*Now* I am,' Rina agreed.

Omar turned and looked again to his son, and he recalled himself striding into the office brandishing files on potential brides. He hoped Felicia had been unable to understand what he had said.

'Kedah showed me a presentation that he has been working on,' Omar said. 'It was very beautiful. In fact, it reminded me of my dreams for Zazinia.' He looked out to the city. 'He has a gift.'

'So do you.'

'Perhaps, but I could not express it properly to my father. Of course back then we did not have the technology to make such a presentation...'

'Nothing would have swayed your father,' Rina said. 'Remember how you tried?'

Omar nodded.

'And then you stopped trying.'

'I chose to focus on the things I *could* change,' Omar said. 'I wanted my bride to be happy. And you weren't.'

'But I am now,' she said. 'And I am much stronger for your love. I shall always have that.'

And then Rina was the bravest she had ever been.

'Come what may.'

Still, even now, they could not properly discuss her infidelity—and not just because of pride or shame, but also because walls might have ears and whispers might multiply.

'Speak to your eldest son, Omar. Now. Before it is too late. Offer him your full support.'

Rina stood after Omar had left and tears were streaming down her face. Oh, she knew how her husband and eldest son protected her, but she was a *good* queen and it was time for the people to come first.

And Rina had not lied.

She *was* stronger for her King's love.

Nothing could take that from her. Even if the law dictated that Omar must shame and divorce her, still she would have his love.

'Kedah?' Omar caught up with son. 'Can I walk with you?'

'Of course,' Kedah answered.

'Your presentation left me speechless. I had never considered using murals on the east-facing walls. It would be an incredible sight.'

'They could tell the tale of our history,' Kedah said. 'Of course scaffolding would be required to shield the beach during construction...'

'We are not at war now,' Omar said. 'Those rules were put in place at a time when the palace risked invasion. I pointed that out to my father many years ago...' He gave a low laugh. 'You are like a mirror image of me. When I see your visions it is like look-ing at my own designs...'

Kedah turned in brief surprise. 'We are nothing alike.'

'Not in looks,' Omar said. 'But we think the same.'

Kedah did not believe it. His father was staid and old-fashioned in his ways.

But Omar pressed on.

'You were right to challenge me in the office. When I studied architecture with Hussain we had such grand plans. My father said that once I had married he would listen to my thoughts. I returned from my honeymoon with so many plans and dreams. Your mother was already pregnant with you, and I can remember us walking along this very beach, talking of the schools and the hospitals that would soon be built. Your mother, being your mother, looked forward to the hotels and the shops. They were such exciting times. There was such an air of hope amongst the people. But even by the time you were born those dreams had died.'

'How?'

'My father preferred his own rules.'

For a moment they stopped walking.

Even though the old King was dead it was almost a forbidden conversation.

'He had always said that when I was married—when I was officially Crown Prince—then I could have input. And so I married. I chose a bride from a progressive country.'

'For that reason only?' Kedah checked.

'He was just delaying things, though. By the time you were born I knew he would never listen to what I had to say. It was a very difficult time…' Omar admitted. 'I was young and proud and I had promised your mother so many things—she had come from a modern country and I wanted the same. I wanted our people to prosper from our wealth too, but my hands were tied. I became very angry and bitter. I spent all my time trying to convince my father to listen to my ideas—travelling with him, pointing out how progressive other countries were. Your mother was in a foreign country with a new baby, but I had no time for either of you...'

They walked in silence as Omar remembered that difficult trip away, and coming home to a grim palace and a wife who had been utterly distraught.

And then had come her confession.

And as Omar remembered the past Kedah better understood his parents, for he could envisage how undermined his father would have felt. For a little while he pondered how he might feel, bringing Felicia here, to a land full of promises that did not come true.

'You have a good marriage now,' Kedah commented.

'We have worked hard to achieve that.' Omar nodded. 'I had been so caught up in my own ego that I forgot what it must be like for your mother...alone in a new country, with no one to speak of her problems with...'

Except Abdal.

'When did you realise you loved her?' Kedah asked—not just because he was curious about his parents' marriage, but because it was a question from his own heart. Suddenly he could not bear to envisage a future without Felicia. Their conversations, their laughter, their occasional rows...he just could not see himself doing those things with anyone else. And yet she was flying further away from him with each moment that passed.

'When?' he asked again, for his father was lost in thought.

Omar was thinking back to the day Rina had confessed what had taken place and his reaction.

'The moment I realised I could lose her,' Omar answered. 'It was then I knew I was in love.'

Perhaps they were not so different after all.

'Your grandfather was not a fan of your mother. He seemed to think I would do better to take another bride.'

Nothing was said outright, but both knew the rumours were finally being addressed.

Kedah could see how things might have happened. Perhaps he understood his mother more. And yet he realised it was not *his* forgiveness that his mother needed.

It was the forgiveness of the man he looked to now.

'Not only did I not want to lose her, Kedah, I was scared for her also.'

Kedah looked at him, and it was then he knew that he was his father's son.

They had the same fears for a vibrant, impetuous woman.

Kedah had never admired his father more, for it took a strong king to be a loving one too—especially when wronged.

'How did you resolve things?' he asked, for he needed his father's wisdom.

'I accepted that my time would one day come and I went back to concentrating on my family. All that time I'd spent fruitlessly clashing with my father I had neglected your mother—and you...'

Here was a man who was far stronger than Kedah had given him credit for.

'You have the same visions I once did,' Omar said. 'But I am older now. I need support. And I do not want you to have to wait, as I did, to make changes. That is not good for the people. Your presentation has reminded me of my own fire. Together we could change things. But there is Mohammed and the elders to consider...'

'You are King.'

'Yes, but there is your mother...'

And Kedah thought of Felicia's words. His mother would be okay. After all, she had the King's love.

'Together,' Kedah said, 'we can protect her.'

So much was said without words.

'But there is a condition,' Kedah said to his father. 'I shall choose my own bride.'

'Perhaps we could wait until after the Accession Council meets?' Omar suggested, for he was quite sure who Kedah's choice would be—which would make for an even more difficult meeting.

But Kedah, now that his decision was made, could no longer wait.

He excused himself from his father and walked

into the palace. As he did so he saw Mohammed walking into his office with Fatiq.

'Mohammed.' Kedah followed him in. 'We need to speak.' He didn't even look over to Fatiq as he addressed him. 'Please leave.'

'You can say what you have to in front of Fatiq,' Mohammed told him.

'Very well.'

The timbre of Kedah's voice was so ominous that Mohammed's hand moved to the hilt of his sword as his elder brother strode towards him.

'Know this. It is very hard to dissuade loyal people... If I am forced to I will take the decision to them and I know I will win.'

'Not if we call for—'

'I don't give a damn about some test that was invented ten minutes ago compared with the rich history of our land. I was born to be King, I was raised to be King. And if I have to I shall take it to the people. Tomorrow my father shall offer his full support for his eldest son, and I hope he shall also announce that I have chosen my bride—Felicia.'

There was a hiss of breath from Fatiq at his side, but instead of an angry response Mohammed gave a black smile.

'The elders would never accept her...'

'They will have no choice.' Omar came in then. 'I will offer my full support.' He glared at the feuding duo. 'Your mother is on her way.'

Rina arrived then, with Kumu.

'Kedah, your father tells me you have exciting news…'

'I *hope* to have exciting news.'

'But Felicia does not understand our ways…the people…' Kumu, who rarely spoke, did so now.

'Felicia understands *people*,' Kedah said. 'Full stop.'

'And our people would adore to see their Crown Prince happy.' Rina smiled. 'Just so long as you are married here.'

'I haven't asked her yet,' Kedah said. 'I think it's a bit early to be speaking of wedding plans.'

'It's never too early,' Rina said.

'And I happen to like a good English wedding,' Omar mused.

And then, just as Kedah was about to roll his eyes and excuse himself, his father took his wife's hand and spoke on.

'What is it they say in the English service? Speak now or for ever hold your peace?'

Omar was looking directly at Mohammed as he said it, and there was challenge in his tone.

Never had Kedah admired his father more.

His father.

Kedah no longer needed proof, for Omar stood proud and strong and he maintained his sovereignty.

'Do you have anything you would like to say, Mohammed?' Omar enquired.

His son blinked.

'Come on, Mohammed.' Kumu pulled at his arm. 'We should go and check on the children.'

Mohammed stood there. They all watched and waited, but it was Kedah who walked off.

He had rather more important things on his mind than waiting for his brother to speak…

Or for ever hold his peace.

CHAPTER FOURTEEN

THERE WAS NO thanking God that it was Friday.

Felicia had deposited the sample at midnight and now all she could do was wait.

Kedah had told her to go in to work as usual. The one thing she didn't have to worry about was money. Felicia had worked hard for many years and commanded an impressive wage. But work was still important to her and, like it or not, Kedah was her boss.

Yes, her boss.

Somehow she had turned into a real PA.

She had rescheduled her meeting with Vadia and knew they would be talking at ten. Before that she had to liaise with the manager at the Dubai hotel and arrange for some signatures from the surveyor.

Felicia chose a boxy little grey suit. She usually saved it for court appearances, but she could use a little power dressing today.

Felicia came out of the underground and walked towards the office, but instead of seeing the doorman smiling at her, she saw he was obscured by the gathered press.

Felicia watched as poor Anu got out of her husband's car and shielded her face.

Finally, after three months, Felicia was being put to work. *This* was the reason she was here and the reason she had been hired, she realised as she stepped in and faced the cameras.

'The proposed hotel in Dubai—will it still go ahead?'

'How will this affect the European branch?'

'Is the Crown Prince stepping aside willingly or is he being forced to stand down?'

Questions were coming from every angle, and Felicia stood there as the microphones and cameras clamoured for a response and did what she did best.

She smiled.

Widely.

'Of course I'll take your questions,' she said, and proceeded to answer them in turn. 'I'm actually just about to speak with the surveyor. Absolutely the sister hotel will be going ahead.'

'Sister?'

'Yes, I believe the new complex is going to focus more on holidaymakers than the business traveller. Next?'

Kedah watched the live stream and knew he had been so right to hire her.

His employees could not be in better hands. She was taking the edge off the fear that would be sweeping through his empire today.

One by one she answered the questions and then, for Felicia, came the hardest of them all.

'Is it correct that his marriage will be announced later today?'

Kedah watched her closely for her response.

It was flawless.

'I'm more than happy to answer, where I can, your questions about the business side of things, but I would never comment on the Sheikh's personal life without his authority.'

'You *must* know...'

'I'm his PA.' Felicia smiled. 'Certainly he doesn't report to *me*.'

With question time over, she smiled at the relieved doorman, who held the door open for her, and took the elevator to the offices on the top floor.

Anu was crying as she walked in, and Felicia knew exactly why she had been hired.

Not for the press but for his staff.

Kedah had made provisions for them even on his darkest day.

'He'll be fine,' she assured Anu.

'You say that for the cameras,' Anu wept. 'But what if they choose Mohammed? Zazinia needs Kedah. We all want him to one day be King. Even when he was a little boy everyone adored him so much, but never more than now.'

And Felicia adored him too.

Which was why, when her heart was breaking, she kept on working. She fired back responses to emails from worried managers and investors the world over, she took phone calls and video calls, and she even managed to hold her composure when Vadia stuck a virtual knife through her heart.

'Whatever the outcome of the Accession Council meeting, there will be an announcement from the palace later tonight as to his chosen bride.'

It was a hellish Friday, made harder when a courier arrived and she had to sign for a plain package. She opened it, and inside there was a thick cream envelope. And, for all that today had been hard, now it tipped into agony.

She blew her nose and put on lip gloss before calling him. She forced her mouth into a smile as she waited for him to answer, because one of the assertiveness courses she had been to had told her it forced a happier and more confident tone.

No matter how fake.

'Hey,' Felicia said at the delicious sound of his voice. 'Your results just arrived.'

'What are you doing?' Kedah asked. 'How has it been?'

'Not too bad. A lot of press and a little bit of panic from some quarters, but it's dying down now.'

'Good.'

'When do the Accession Council meet?' Felicia asked, wondering why he didn't have her tearing the envelope open now.

'An hour or so,' he said, as if it hardly mattered. 'I want to ask you something. What did you say to

Kumu on the stairs? She hasn't been quite the same since!'

Felicia let out a low chuckle. 'I just pointed out that, as nice as your father is, he's still King and he clearly loves his wife. I said that I'd *hate* to offend him.'

He laughed, and then he was serious. 'Are you going to open it?'

'Sure,' she said. 'I'm just going to put you down.'

She placed the phone on the desk and put him on speaker, and then she took out a letter opener and sliced open the envelope.

Kedah listened carefully. There were no sniffles or heavy breathing. Felicia was indeed tough.

'Congratulations, Your Royal Highness.'

She smiled, and it was a genuine one.

No, she didn't want him to be King—but that was a selfish wish. She was also terribly pleased for him.

'Go get 'em,' she said.

'Hey, Felicia…?'

'I have to go, Kedah,' she said.

'You can talk for a moment.'

'No.' She smiled again. 'I really do have to go. Good luck!'

Absolutely she had to go. Because she was starting to break down.

He didn't need to know as he went into a fight for the throne that she loved him and would do so for ever. And neither did he need to be sideswiped by the news that she was pregnant.

In time she would tell him—somehow.

Yet she knew she was tough and could raise their child alone.

She thought of all the people who loved their Prince and needed change.

She just needed a moment to cry. And she put her head in her hands and sat at her desk to weep in a way she never had.

Oh, Felicia had cried before—of course she had— but she sobbed now.

There was no need to worry about Anu hearing, for Felicia's sobs were deep and quiet and racked her body. She wrapped her arms around herself, scared that if she let go she might fall apart.

She was so deep in grief that she didn't hear the door open.

'Felicia...'

His voice stilled her.

Kedah had been sure of her love, but as he'd watched her on the live stream and heard her speak on the phone moments before she had sounded so composed that for a moment his certainty had wavered.

She looked up, stood up, and there were so many questions.

'You should be there...' she said, and there was no way to hide her tears so she ran to him.

He held her tight in his arms and Kedah knew he had been right to return when he had. Sometimes you had to look after those you loved first.

'I'm not needed there. My father will go in and tell them who is the rightful Crown Prince...' He held her closer. 'But I *am* needed here...'

He kissed her, and there were so many things that he wanted to say, but right now not one of them mattered.

It was a kiss so deep and so passionate that it should never have ended, and yet there were too many things she needed to know.

And Kedah too.

'Were you crying the morning I called you and you said that you had a cold?'

Felicia nodded.

'I have spoken with my father. I have told him that I have chosen my bride...'

And as she winced, as she braced herself to hear the chosen name, he pulled out a diamond that was familiar. He told her that soon it would be mounted on gold and worn on her finger.

'Every time I looked at this I knew I would be okay, and I want the same for you...'

The diamond had reassured him that come what may he would be taken care of, and in handing it over to Felicia he afforded her the same reassurance.

'Marry me?'

Never in her wildest dreams had she thought she might hear those words from Kedah.

Liar.

Had his driver been there he might have stood and applauded—and, yes, she might have joined in.

For, yes, in her wildest dreams she *had* hoped that one day he would say those words, that there might somehow be hope for them.

'I didn't want you to be your father's son.' It was a terrible confession to make. 'I feel so guilty, because I've been hoping and wishing that you weren't because then there might be a chance for *us*...'

'I make my own chances, Felicia, and there is no need to feel guilty. I am glad that you wanted a chance for us.' He thought back to Mohammed's cruel words. 'It is wonderful that you love me whether or not I might one day be King.'

It would make her a princess, who would one day be Queen, and an extremely worrying thought occurred.

'Kedah, there's going to be the most terrible scandal...' Even if they married this week there would always be a question over the dates. 'I'm pregnant...'

She was starting to panic, for no spin doctor could fix this—no dates could be changed—and it would be she, Felicia, who brought discredit to his name.

Yet Kedah smiled. 'Really?'

'I took a test. They're going to know that we...'

'Felicia.' Kedah still smiled. 'If my people are going to be shocked that we have slept together, that I am not a virgin, then they don't know me at all.'

He made her laugh through her tears.

'But they *do* know me, and they care for me—just as they will care for you.'

'You're not cross?'

'Cross? I am stunned, I am thrilled and I am scared that you might not have told me.'

'I was trying to work out how.'

'Together we will sort out our problems,' he said. 'And right now I can't see that we have any. Can you?'

Felicia thought for a moment, but not long and hard.

Oh, there would surely be problems, but they would deal with them together.

She could cope with anything.

After all, she had Kedah's love.

EPILOGUE

SHE WOULD ALWAYS express her opinion.

Though occasionally, Felicia conceded, only to herself, she did get it wrong.

His work was stunning, and nowhere more so than here in the palace.

There were now no offices in the Crown Prince's wing. Kedah had indeed had them torn down. They had been replaced by walls of soft stone from the quarries, and a trickling noise lined them, coming from the soft fountains from a deep spring the diviner had found.

The sound soothed both Felicia and the baby she sat with this dawn. It felt as if she was sitting in a blissful sanctuary.

'You've got a big day today,' Felicia said to her daughter.

Yes, they had been gifted with a little girl.

She had been born eight months ago, and her public appearances since then had been brief. She had been tiny enough to sleep through them, but she was bigger now—a bit more dramatic and clingy. Felicia was worried about how she would react to the crowds.

Kaina.

It meant both *female* and *leader*, and her name spoke of another of the changes that had been made.

She would one day be Queen of this magnificent land. But for now she was just a baby who really needed to sleep—except she had other ideas.

Kaina's long eyelashes were just closing when the gap in the half-open door widened, and Felicia watched as her daughter's little head turned.

'She was nearly asleep,' Felicia said as the baby smiled and wriggled and held out her arms.

'Go back to bed,' Kedah said as he took their daughter from her, for Felicia had been up for ages and he knew that she was worried about today.

'She's been fed,' Felicia said. 'She just won't settle.'

'Go back to bed,' he said again. 'I'll get her to sleep.'

He didn't suggest calling the royal nanny. Felicia was having none of that. And neither did their daughter sleep in a separate wing from her parents.

Times had finally changed, she thought as she climbed into their magnificent bed and closed her eyes.

And the landscape had changed also.

Kedah held his daughter and watched as the sun started to rise over Zazinia. A hotel had already been built and it was the most stunning building—his proudest work. No windows looked to the palace. Instead there was a beautiful mural that told some of the history of Zazinia. And close to the hotel in the modern city he was creating were the beginnings of a hospital, built with stone from the quarries of Zazinia but gleaming and modern inside. It was already functioning, but it would be a couple more years until it was complete.

'Today,' Kedah said, and he spoke in a low voice to his daughter, 'there are going to be a lot of people cheering and making noise…'

He didn't tell her that she was to behave and not cry. Of course Kaina was too young to understand, but there were other rules he had changed. Kaina would be herself, and go to school with her peers.

He looked down at his precious daughter, who was finally asleep, and walked out of the dark sanctuary and placed her in her crib.

There were no portraits on the wall as he walked back to his suite.

They were for the formal corridors now.

Here was home.

And home was a palace, and today the people would gather to see their beloved royals.

'You're going to be fine,' Kedah said to Felicia, who was very nervous.

Oh, she had faced angry press many times in her past, but facing these people was different. The men she had represented in the past had meant absolutely nothing to her.

This man did.

Her robe was that certain shade of green which brought out the best in her eyes, and Kedah had chosen white for today. He looked sultry and sexy, and the only thing marriage had done to tone him down was to direct all that passion to one woman.

'Felicia!'

Rina was chatting to Mohammed and Kumu as Felicia approached, but she was overtaken by a tiny little boy who had just found his feet.

'Abi…'

He called for his father and Felicia watched as Mohammed's austere face broke into a smile as his youngest son toddled over and Mohammed scooped him up.

For Mohammed was his father's son also.

When he had accepted that there was nothing he could do to change the lineage, instead of plotting bitterly he had chosen to focus on what he could do best. He had always loved his wife and children, and now he let it show.

And he had worked with Kedah to build a new Zazinia, and Kedah respected his brother's sage advice.

'I like it that the portraits are here by the main balcony…' Rina said. 'My husband hated standing for his. And look at Kedah!' Rina suddenly laughed. 'He looks nothing like the rest of them…'

Oblivious.

Rina had been coddled, shielded from the fact that everyone knew her secret—the terrible mistake she had made many years ago. To this day she thought only her husband knew about that week many years ago, when Omar had been away, and lost and lonely she had turned to the wrong man for comfort. But he had brought none.

'Really,' Rina said, with all the assuredness of someone who had *not* been having an affair around conception time, 'Kedah doesn't even look related. He takes after my side of the family, of course...'

And Felicia caught Kumu's eyes and both women shared a smile.

They loved Queen Rina. Yes, she was dramatic and flaky, but she was also the kindest woman— even if at times she ran a little wild.

Like her eldest son.

'We should go out now,' Omar said.

The King loathed these formal moments. His whole life had been spent being told to behave or to keep his family in check.

Today they all walked out to loud cheers.

Kaina was startled, and Felicia hushed her, but of course she started to cry.

'Give her to me,' Rina said. 'So you can wave. It is you they all want to see.'

No, it wasn't.

The crowd cheered as their lovely Queen took the little baby, and they cheered more loudly on seeing Omar looking so happy and relaxed.

And then they called out for Kedah.

He waved and he smiled. He was so proud of his lovely wife, and the people just adored him.

They loved the way he came down to the quarries and spoke with the workers, how when the hospital had opened he had stayed for hours to meet with the staff.

Kaina was really crying now, and refused to be held in Rina's arms. Kedah took his daughter and held her so she was sitting on his hip. And Kaina, safe in her daddy's arms, buried her face in his chest.

But then she peeked out.

To see all the people.

There were so many that she put her little hand over her eyes, so she didn't have to see them, and then she put her hand down and saw they were still there.

And they were laughing.

So she put her hand over her eyes again.

Oh, indeed she was her father's daughter.

She was playing peekaboo with the crowd, and from this day on she would hold them in the palm of her hand.

'You,' Kedah said to little Kaina as they headed inside, 'were amazing.'

The nanny came and took her. Kaina would go and play rather than sit through a long formal lunch.

There was an hour, though, before they had to be seated, and Felicia wandered off to stand by the portraits.

The old artist was working on a portrait of little Kaina now.

All the portraits fascinated her, but one especially so.

She didn't turn as Kedah joined her. 'You *are* smiling.'

'No.'

They had argued about it often, but there amongst the stern faces of Crown Princes of old, she knew one stood out—and not just because of his attire. There was a certain Mona Lisa smile on Kedah's face, though he repeatedly denied it.

'Yes, you are,' Felicia insisted.

'I like your robe.' He did his best to change the subject. 'I love that shade of green.'

'I know you do.'

'We have forty minutes before we have to go through. Perhaps we should check on Kaina.'

'Kaina's fine.'

'We could make sure,' he said, and then he looked up at the portrait and conceded defeat. 'I was thinking of *you*,' he said in her ear, and Felicia resisted turning. 'And what had happened on the plane.'

She turned then, and looked into the eyes of the only man she had ever loved.

'Come on,' Kedah said.

There was love to be made.

* * * * *